Amanda Grange lives in Cheshire.

STORMCROW CASTLE

On visiting Stormcrow Castle, Helena Carlisle is disturbed to find that her aunt, the housekeeper, has disappeared. Helena takes on the role of the new housekeeper, but it is not long before strange incidents begin to unnerve her. The castle's owner, Simon, Lord Torkrow, frequents the graveyard at night; the portrait gallery conceals a secret room; identities are hidden at a masked ball; and the key to the attic is missing. As the secrets unravel, Helena finds herself drawn into a world where nothing is as it seems, and she must fight for her chance of love . . . and to survive.

Books by Amanda Grange
Published by The House of Ulverscroft:

THE SIX-MONTH MARRIAGE
CARISBROOKE ABBEY
HARSTAIRS HOUSE

AMANDA GRANGE

STORMCROW CASTLE

Complete and Unabridged

ULVERSCROFT
Leicester

First published in Great Britain in 2007 by
Robert Hale Limited
London

First Large Print Edition
published 2008
by arrangement with
Robert Hale Limited
London

British Library CIP Data

Grange, Amanda
    Stormcrow Castle.—Large print ed.—
    Ulverscroft large print series: romantic suspense
    1. Young women—England—Fiction 2. Women
    domestics—England—Fiction 3. England—Social life
    and customs—19th century—Fiction 4. Romantic
    suspense novels 5. Large type books
    I. Title
    823.9'2 [F]

    ISBN 978–1–84782–058–7

Published by
F. A. Thorpe (Publishing)
Anstey, Leicestershire

Set by Words & Graphics Ltd.
Anstey, Leicestershire
Printed and bound in Great Britain by
T. J. International Ltd., Padstow, Cornwall

This book is printed on acid-free paper

1

Helena Carlisle rested her valise on the dry stone wall and peered into the gathering gloom. The March daylight was fading and she was beginning to feel uneasy. The carrier had told her it was only two miles to Stormcrow Castle but she had already walked three miles across the moor. She strained her eyes but there was no sign of the castle, nor was there any sign of a house at which she could ask for directions. Looking over her shoulder, she wondered if she should retrace her steps, but it was a long way back to the nearest town and she decided to continue on her way. She picked up her valise and walked along the rutted road, bending her head against the icy wind and praying it would not snow.

A sound disturbed the silence and, looking back, she saw a speck in the distance. As it drew closer she could see that it was a coach, racing towards her. Four black horses were pulling it, and it was swaying from side to side. She stepped aside to let it pass, but, as it drew level with her, the horses were reined in and the coach rolled to an abrupt halt. The door was flung open and a man's voice said, 'Get in.'

She was about to back away when she caught sight of the gentleman inside. She heard her aunt's voice in her memory: 'Like a portrait, he is, with his gaunt face and his long, pointed chin. He should have been living in 1619, not 1819. Lord Torkrow his name is, but no one calls him that hereabouts. They all call him Stormcrow.'

'Don't dawdle, you're late as it is,' he snapped.

Late? she thought uneasily. *But I didn't tell anyone I was coming.*

'Well?' he demanded.

She hesitated, but she had to reach the castle and, as she was already weary, she lifted the hem of her cloak and climbed inside. He slammed the door shut and rapped on the floor with his cane, then the coach pulled away, quickly building up speed and racing on again.

As she settled herself opposite him, Helena regarded Lord Torkrow covertly. He had no pretensions to being handsome. His face was thin and sharp, and his eyes looked as though they held secrets.

'Well?' he asked suddenly. 'Does my visage please you?'

Helena realized she had been staring.

'It is . . . '

He raised one eyebrow in silent challenge.

' . . . striking,' she finished.

His lips curled. 'A good choice of word. It means precisely nothing. But let it pass.' He regarded her appraisingly. 'You're very young to be a housekeeper.'

'A housekeeper?' she asked, startled.

'I have been waiting two weeks for the registry office to send me a replacement. They have been very lax. If they do not do better in future, I shall use Jensen's office instead.'

She felt a cold chill, and pulled her cloak about her. Why did he think she was a housekeeper? Her aunt was the housekeeper at Stormcrow Castle.

'The registry office did tell you the vacancy was for a housekeeper? Or did they describe the post as a chatelaine?' he asked with a grimace. 'If you are imagining the castle to be a fashionable establishment, you will be sorely disappointed. There are no fine rooms; no army of servants; no touring visitors calling at the doors and begging to be shown round.'

'But I thought Mrs Carlisle was your housekeeper?' she said cautiously, wondering if she had mistaken him, and he was not Lord Torkrow after all.

'They have sent me a half-wit!' he muttered under his breath, then out loud he said, 'Mrs Carlisle left my service. She went to nurse her sister and will not be returning. That is why I need a replacement.'

Helena felt disoriented. Her aunt could not possibly have left to nurse her sister, for she did not have a sister.

'You do have experience as a housekeeper?' he asked.

'Yes,' said Helena, recalling the six months she had spent working for Mr and Mrs Hamilton, before they had left the country and removed to Wales.

'That is something, at least. You should have been here yesterday.'

She remained silent, considering what to say. If she revealed who she was then she would learn nothing more, for he had already told her that her aunt had left his service, and he would stop the carriage and expect her to return to town. But if she went to the castle in the guise of the new housekeeper, then she would have an opportunity to speak to the other servants and perhaps learn more about her aunt's sudden departure.

'No matter,' he said, 'you are here now.'

He leant back against the red squabs and his cloak spread across them like a cloud blotting out the sun.

The coach lurched as it turned off the main road and on to a narrow track. She glanced out of the window, but there was nothing to be seen; nothing but the endless expanse of moor, gradually losing all colour in the fading light. At last the coach began to slow its pace. Up ahead, she dimly perceived the outline of a high stone wall, and then they were plunged into darkness as the coach passed beneath an archway. She felt her hands grow clammy. One heartbeat . . . two . . . three . . . then the darkness lifted and they emerged into a courtyard. A gravel road encircled a patch of lawn which might once have been fine, but which had now grown wild. Coarse grass had embedded itself there, as the moor had encroached on the civilized world.

'We're almost there,' he said.

The coach finally rolled to a halt. The coachman opened the door and lowered the step. Lord Torkrow climbed out. Helena followed him, and looked up at the forbidding walls of Stormcrow Castle.

It was a long, low building with a central square turret and two wings arranged symmetrically on either side. The door was arched, and above it there was a sickly yellow light, shining from a rose window. Crenellations ran along the top of the roof, thrusting their way into the sky like broken teeth.

Helena felt a frisson of anxiety. There was an atmosphere surrounding the castle. Isolated and exposed, it seemed malevolent, and she shivered, reluctant to go inside.

'Cold?' he asked.

'A little,' she said, trying to speak bravely.

'It's colder inside.'

With these words he led her up to the door. Without waiting for a servant to open it he seized the iron ring and turned it, then pushed the heavy oak door inwards. He disappeared into the gloom and she followed him, finding herself in a cavernous hall with tapestries decorating the walls, and a huge fireplace, which was large enough to swallow her whole. The floor was bare, and was made of massive stone flags, discoloured with centuries of use.

'You will have plenty to do,' he said, taking a candelabra from a table next to the fireplace and removing one of the candles, putting it into a separate holder before handing it to her. 'The castle has been neglected for some time.'

Helena looked at the thick dust on the table and wondered how long it was since her aunt had left.

'Follow me,' he said.

His cloak stirred as it was caught by a draught, and it billowed around him as he set off at a brisk pace across the hall. The candles were small haloes of light in the gloom, revealing the dim outlines of suits of armour, plated and riveted in the semblance of men, gleaming dully in the fading light. Their silver was darkened with age and fantastic beasts were embossed on their breast plates, whilst above them hung weapons and shields. They had a sullen look about them, as though they resented the fact they were no longer used, like savage animals that had been caged.

Helena turned her head away from the warlike sight and looked straight ahead, but it was little better, for the cavernous space was ominous and she felt suddenly very small. Above her, the ceiling was too high to be seen. Lord Torkrow expected her to match his pace and she had to run to keep up with him.

At the far end of the hall they came to a massive stone staircase. The steps were wide and shallow, worn to a hollow in the centre with the passage of countless feet, and they led upwards into the darkness.

Lord Torkrow began to climb, and Helena followed. Her legs felt like lead long before she reached the top, for the steps were numerous, and she had already walked a long way that day. She paused to rest at the top, but a curt 'Don't dawdle', set her hurrying after the earl again.

He turned left and led her along an ice-cold corridor, and then stopped abruptly at a door that blocked their way. It was forbidding, made of blackened oak and studded with iron.

'Your room is through the door and at the end of the corridor,' he said. 'You will wait upon me in the library at six o'clock, when we will discuss your previous experience, and I will instruct you in your duties, after which you may return to your own room and rest. Tomorrow you will start work in earnest.'

Helena opened her mouth to reply, but before she could say anything, he turned on his heel and disappeared into the shadows.

A drop of hot wax fell on to her hand, returning her thoughts to her own situation, and she was glad she was wearing gloves, for if her hands had been bare it would have burnt her.

It was a very irregular household, she thought, as she opened the door. There had been no servant to open the door, no footmen waiting in the hall, and no maid to show her to her room. Even more irregularly, his lordship had shown her the way himself, and seemed to be intent on giving her her instructions. There was no lady of the house, then. Feeling the chill from the old stone, she was not surprised. What lady would want to bury herself in a dank castle on the moors, with a dark and brooding man for a husband? Earl or no earl, he was the sort of man to strike terror into the heart, rather than any softer emotion.

She went through the door, knowing at once she was in the servants' part of the house, for there were no tapestries hanging on the wall. She was in a narrow passage with windows to her left, looking out on to the side of the castle, whilst to her right was a row of doors. At the end of the corridor was a final oak door which, gathering her courage, she opened. It was heavy, and it creaked as it moved, making her shiver. As she went in, ghostly shapes loomed out of the darkness, and, through the window she saw the moor looking bleak and dour. She had never seen such darkness before. In her rented room in Manchester there had always been a candle in a neighbouring window, or a glow from a nearby inn, or a flambeau on the street below. But here there was nothing; nothing but impenetrable blackness, unalleviated by a star or a sliver of moon.

Feeling suddenly afraid, she dropped her valise and quickly pulled the heavy curtains across the window, then hurriedly lit every candle in the room. As the flames sprang to life, the ghostly shapes resolved themselves into pieces of furniture that sat, squat and heavy, in the darkly panelled chamber. There was a four-poster bed with dark-red curtains, a large oak cupboard, a carved washstand, a cheval glass and, over by the empty grate, a table and chair.

She went over to the table and put her candlestick down. Was this where Aunt Hester had written her letters? she wondered. The surface was scored and pock-marked; it looked very old.

Overcome with a sudden loneliness, she took paper, ink, sand and a quill from her valise and sat down at the desk. Pulling off her gloves, she dipped the quill in the ink, and began to write.

My dear Caroline,

I have arrived at Stormcrow Castle, but something unsettling has happened. I have discovered that my aunt is no longer here, and, even worse, Lord Torkrow has mistaken me for the new housekeeper. I cannot think where Aunt Hester has gone. Lord Torkrow says she left to look after a sick sister, but she does not have a sister. Why did she lie to him? And where is she?

I, too, have lied, for I have allowed him to think I am the housekeeper he was expecting. I am not easy about it. It does not sit well with my conscience, but I wanted to find out more about Aunt Hester's strange departure, and I could think of no other way. I hope to question the other servants, and, having done so, I will return to Manchester.

I will probably not post this letter. There do not seem to be many servants in the castle, and I might be able to speak to them all tomorrow, returning to Manchester before you could receive it, but I wanted to write because it makes me feel you are near, and I need to feel I have a friend. The castle is cold and dark, and it is taking all of my courage not to be afraid.

But enough of me. I hope you had good luck with Mrs Ling, and that you are now her new companion. You certainly deserve the position, but positions, alas, do not always go to those who deserve them. What a trial it is for us both, to be constantly having to seek work!

I know what you would say, that I should accept Mr Gradwell, but I am not sure I want to marry a man I do not love. That is why I need Aunt Hester's counsel.

I am worried, Caroline. She is all I have in the world, except you, my dear friend. Where can she have gone?

The faint sound of chimes from a far-away clock reached her ears. It was five o'clock. She had an hour before she had to see Lord Torkrow. Her stomach began to growl, reminding her that she had not eaten since that morning, and she resolved to find the kitchen and ask for something to eat.

I can write no more at present, but I hope to be with you before long.
Your affectionate friend,
Helena

She sanded the letter, then folded it and put it in the pocket of her gown, glad to have it with her, for it reminded her that Caroline was not too far away. Then, removing her pelisse and bonnet she picked up her candle and went out into the corridor.

The cook is Mrs Beal, she reminded herself, as she went in search of the stairs down to the kitchen. The cold from the stone floor bit into her feet, even through the soles of her shoes, and icy draughts lifted the hem of her gown. She walked briskly, feeling some welcome warmth creep into her body with the exercise, and was relieved when she saw the top of a back staircase. She went down the stairs, finding them narrower than those in the hall for, being used by servants, they had no need to be imposing.

She had never been in such an old building before, and the size of it was daunting. Down, down went the steps, and the walls were shrouded in shadows. Her footsteps had an eerie sound in the vastness, and she had to tell herself that the *tap, tap* following her was nothing but an echo of her own footsteps. Even so, twice she glanced over her shoulder, convinced that someone was following her. The second time, she thought she saw the hem of a gown pulling back into the shadows, but when she turned round and lifted her candle high, there was no one there.

Unnerved by the incident, she ran down the rest of the steps, but at the bottom she was forced to stop, because she was not sure which way to turn. She peered ahead into the gloom. In the distance, to her left, she saw what appeared to be the top of another flight of steps. She went over to them and descended once more, lifting her skirt in one hand and treading carefully, for the stone was smooth and slippery. She emerged in another corridor, and the smell of damp that had pervaded the stairwell was replaced by the smell of baking coming from a door in front of her. The warm, inviting scent lifted her spirits as she opened the door.

The kitchen was clean and well cared for.

The table was scrubbed, the floor was gleaming, and copper pots and pans glowed red in the firelight.

Mrs Beal knows her business, Helena thought. Her eyes ran over a large woman of ample girth, who was standing at the kitchen table. She was wearing a clean dress protected by a floury apron; her sleeves were rolled up to her elbows, and she was busy kneading some pastry.

'Well,' said Mrs Beal, looking up, 'so you're here at last! I've set the kettle over the fire. I knew you'd be cold.'

'How did you know I'd arrived?' asked Helena.

'Effie saw you,' she said, glancing at the scullery maid who was peeling potatoes in the corner.

She spoke cheerfully, and Helena felt that here was someone who might be able and willing to help her discover what had become of her aunt.

'You'll be wanting something to eat,' went on Mrs Beal, knocking her hands together to remove the flour before wiping them on her apron. 'Leave those, Effie, and set the cups out on the table,' she said.

Effie did as she was instructed, and the cook said, 'I'm Mrs Beal. I'm pleased you're here. We've been without a housekeeper for

14

far too long. A place like this quickly gets disordered when there's no one to see to it. The pie'll be out of the oven in a few minutes and it'll do you good. You've had a long journey, I suppose?'

'Yes, I've been travelling all day.'

'And you'll have walked from the stage. It's a fair step, especially in the winter, with the wind whipping across the moor and the ground hard underfoot. You're lucky it didn't snow.'

Helena shivered, and Mrs Beale looked at her critically.

'You're even colder than I thought,' she said. 'Never mind tea, you'd better have some mulled wine. There's nothing like a mug of mulled wine to put new heart into you.'

She took a pitcher from the dresser and put it on the table, where the scents of cinnamon, cloves and nutmeg soon mingled with the scent of the wine. Taking the poker from its place by the fire, she plunged it into the wine and then poured the steaming drink into a mug. Helena took it gratefully, cupping her hands round it and feeling it warming her fingers. She took a sip, and felt the aromatic drink beginning to revive her.

As she began to relax, she wondered if she should take Mrs Beal into her confidence, and reveal that she was Mrs Carlisle's niece, but then she decided against it, for Mrs Beal might feel obliged to tell Lord Torkrow.

'It seems a strange household,' said Helena, as she watched Mrs Beal work. 'Lord Torkrow took me up in his carriage and then, when we arrived at the castle, he opened the door himself. He led me upstairs and told me where to find my room, and he means to instruct me in my duties. Has it always been this way?'

'There's usually a footman to open the door, but today's his afternoon off. We used to have a couple of maids, but they left soon after Mrs Carlisle had gone. They didn't like to be upstairs without a housekeeper.'

'Oh? Why not?' asked Helena.

'There's things said about his lordship in the village. Stuff and nonsense, it is, all of it, but girls will be girls, and if they're not hearing noises, they're seeing things out of the corner of their eyes. Their fathers didn't like it, either, having their daughters here without a housekeeper. Always thinking something's going on, are people in a village.'

From Mrs Beal's demeanour, it was clear that she did not think there was anything going on, and remembering Lord Torkrow's cold manner, Helena could not imagine it, either.

'Of course, it was different in the old days,

when his lordship's father was alive. Then the castle was full of servants: footmen, maids, valets, page boys, kitchen maids, hall boys . . . ' She looked around the table as if seeing it surrounded by servants. 'Jolly it was, at mealtimes. It's much quieter now.'

'Did his lordship dismiss the servants?' asked Helena.

'Ah, well,' said Mrs Beal, suddenly less forthcoming. 'Things change.' She got up and went over to the oven. 'I'm ready for a bit of something myself,' she said, as she took out the pie.

Helena looked at it longingly. The crust was a golden brown, and it smelled savoury.

Mrs Beal was about to sit down, when she appeared to remember herself and went on, 'But perhaps you'd prefer to eat in the housekeeper's room?'

Helena looked round. With its cheery fire and its air of wholesomeness, the kitchen was an inviting place. Besides, she hoped to learn something of use.

'No, I would far rather eat here with you.'

'It's nice to have a bit of company,' said Mrs Beal comfortably.

'Did the last housekeeper eat with you?' asked Helena, reminding herself that she was not meant to have known Mrs Carlisle, and that she must speak of her aunt only in the most general terms.

'Sometimes. She liked to take her breakfast in the kitchen with me,' said Mrs Beal, cutting the pie and putting a generous slice on to Helena's plate. Steam rose from it, and gravy ran round the plate, whilst large chunks of beef fell out of the pastry casing, with pieces of carrots and turnips.

'It must have been difficult for you since Mrs Carlisle left,' she said, sitting opposite Mrs Beal and taking up her fork.

'I won't deny it,' said the cook. 'I've had to do all the ordering and planning myself. Not that I didn't do a lot when Mrs Carlisle was here, but we shared it, and it was always useful to have someone to ask about the menus.'

'She left in a hurry, I understand,' said Helena, as she put a mouthful of the pie into her mouth. The pastry was light and feathery, and the meat was tender, for Mrs Beal was a very good cook.

'Yes, poor lady. It was her sister. She was taken ill. What could Mrs Carlisle do but go and look after her? One night she was drinking chocolate by the fire with me, the next morning she'd left the castle.'

'She left overnight?' asked Helena, putting her fork down in surprise.

'It was on account of the letter that came,'

said Mrs Beal as she, too, ate her meal.

'A letter came late at night?' queried Helena.

Mrs Beal looked surprised. 'That does seem odd, now you mention it. It must have come earlier in the day, of course, but likely she didn't have time to read it. There's always a lot of work in the castle, and she was kept busy.'

'It must have been a comfort for her to be able to talk to you about it,' said Helena.

Mrs Beal shook her head. 'She never mentioned it to me. I would have comforted her if I could have done, but I never saw her. She left before daybreak. It was his lordship who told me about it.'

Helena found the story more and more disturbing.

'She must have had a long walk over the moor. It can't have been pleasant for her in the dark. I hope she didn't miss her way,' she said, hoping to lead Mrs Beal to say more.

'His lordship ordered the carriage for her. He sent her to Draycot, so she could pick up the stagecoach from there.'

'That was very good of him.'

'There's things said about him in the village,' said Mrs Beal, between mouthfuls of pie, 'and of course there was . . . yes, well, least said soonest mended . . . but I've never had anything but kindness from him. There's many a master would have washed their hands of a housekeeper, once she'd decided to leave.'

Helena did not like the sound of *yes, well, least said soonest mended* but for the present she was more interested in her aunt.

'Did she have far to travel?' she asked, trying to sound as though hers was a casual interest.

'I don't rightly know. He didn't say. 'If I'd known, I'd have packed her up a hamper', I said. 'I could have put her up some bread and cheese, and a piece or two of chicken, and some of my apple pie.' I'd made one that morning, and it would have helped her on her way,' she told Helena. 'But the poor lady went off with nothing. I've often wondered about her, and how she's getting on.'

'She has not written to you to let you know that she is all right, and to tell you how her sister is?'

'She won't have time for writing, any more than I have time for reading. Although she did write letters now and again.'

'Yes?' asked Helena, her pulse quickening.

'Yes, to her niece. 'She's all I have in the world', she used to say to me. A nice girl, by all accounts.'

'That was a strange thing to say, if she also

had a sister,' said Helena.

Mrs Beal looked surprised. 'So it was. She must have meant, all I have in the world beside a sister.'

Helena said nothing. It was becoming clear to her that, although Mrs Beal was very friendly, she did not have an enquiring mind. Thoughts of where the housekeeper had gone and what she was doing had not troubled her. She simply accepted what she had been told.

'And she did not tell you she was leaving before she went?' asked Helena. 'How very strange.'

'Folks do strange things when they're upset,' said Mrs Beal sagely. 'My sister once took the cat with her when her daughter was knocked down by a carriage. She meant to put a cushion in the basket, but she took Pussy Willow instead.'

Helena ate her pie and finished her wine, feeling, first of all her limbs, and then her fingers and toes grow warm, and the conversation turned to more practical matters. Mrs Beal told her about the castle, and gave her instructions on how to find the main rooms. As they talked of the housekeeper's room, Helena learnt that, although Mrs Carlisle had taken breakfast and dinner every day with Mrs Beal in the kitchen, she had had her lunch served in the housekeeper's room.

'I think I, too, will take lunch in the housekeeper's room,' said Helena.

She would be sure of one hot meal on the morrow, before she had to face the moor again.

'If you want a dish of tea at any time, just ring the bell. Effie will answer it.'

The scullery maid looked up briefly at the mention of her name, and then went back to peeling the potatoes.

'You'll have a bit of apple dumpling?' asked Mrs Beal, when they had finished their conversation.

Helena readily accepted, and by the time the clock struck a quarter to the hour she was feeling almost cheerful.

'I ought to be going to the library. I have to see his lordship there at six o'clock, and it may take me some time to find it.'

'Effie can show you the way.' Mrs Beal turned round, but Effie was no longer there. 'Never here when wanted,' said Mrs Beal. 'She must've gone to mend the fires. But you'll soon find the library. Just go up to the hall as I said, and it's on your left.'

Taking up a candle, Helena ventured out into the cold corridor once more, but as soon as the kitchen door closed behind her, some of her confidence began to leave her. She felt the cold bite into her, and she was glad of her shawl. After the light of many candles and the glow of the fire, the corridor seemed darker and colder than ever. She hurried along, tripping once on an uneven flagstone, and afterwards not knowing whether to watch her feet, or look at the way ahead. She had an urge to do neither, but instead to look over her shoulder, for she felt sure that someone was following her, but every time she turned round, there was no one there.

It is just my imagination, she told herself, I must not succumb to fancy. But the shadows danced beyond the light of her candle flame, and seemed to mock her with their shifting presence, assuming monstrous shapes before diminishing as she passed.

She came at last to the end of the corridor and went up the steps, and was soon crossing the hall. She counted the doors to her left, then stopped outside the library door as the clock chimed the hour. She smoothed her hair, arranged the folds of her skirt, took a deep breath, and knocked on the door.

2

There was a moment's silence and then the earl's voice called, 'Come in.'

Helena opened the door and found herself in a large room, its walls decorated with hangings and its stone floor covered with a rug. Two candelabras on the mantelpiece and another one on a large desk in the middle of the room did their best to provide light, but the walls were lost in darkness, save for glints of gold coming from the shadows that hinted the room was lined with books. There was a leaping fire in the grate, and in front of it stood the earl, holding a letter in his hand. He looked up as she entered.

'When I ask to see you in future, I expect you to arrive before the last chime has been struck. I will not tolerate tardiness,' he said.

Helena said nothing, not knowing what to reply.

'Well, come in,' he said.

She closed the door and stepped forward.

'So. Mrs Elizabeth Reynolds,' he said, looking down at the letter. 'You have three years' experience of housekeeping, two with the Right Honourable Mrs Keily, and one

24

with the Revd James Plumley. Mr Keily was in business, I see.'

An expression of fastidious distaste crossed his face as he said it, and she was forcibly reminded of the fact that he was an aristocrat. He had never had to earn his living, never known the fear of having nowhere to live, nowhere to go. She imagined a long line of ancestors stretching out behind him, reaching back through the centuries, governing the land and living in the castle. How long had he and his family lived there, she wondered, maintaining tradition, keeping the peace, ruling the neighbourhood? A hundred years? Two hundred years? Or even longer?

He went on, recalling her thoughts.

'You came by your position with Mr Plumley through the registry office, I see,' he said, referring to the letter. 'You wrote to the office again when Mr Plumley married, because his wife chose to manage the house herself, and the office recommended you for the job at the castle.'

'Yes, my lord.'

'Well, you will find it very different here. A castle is not a tradesman's house or a vicarage, even one as lost as this.'

'No, my lord.'

'Now, to your duties. You will make sure the dining-room and the other inhabited rooms are kept clean and warm. You will make sure there is a fire in the library at all times, and you will tend to it yourself. You will not allow any other member of staff to enter the library, except Miss Parkins.'

'Miss Parkins?'

'You will meet her later. She has my full confidence. You will take responsibility for everything that goes on inside the castle and you will make sure that I am not troubled with household matters, except for an appointed hour once a week, when you will report to me. As this is your first week, you will report to me tomorrow afternoon at four o'clock, when I will answer any questions that might have arisen once you have had an opportunity to familiarize yourself with the castle.'

'Very good, my lord.'

'You know enough to begin with.' He waved his hand and said: 'That will be all for today.'

It was a dismissal. Helena inclined her head, then left the room.

As she closed the door behind her, she let out a sigh of relief, for she had passed the test, and been accepted as Elizabeth Reynolds.

She crossed the hall and mounted the stairs, returning to her room. I can do no more this evening, she thought, but tomorrow I must question the footman.

As she opened the door, she felt a welcome heat, and realized that a fire had been lit in her absence. She was about to cross to the fireplace when she saw, with a start, that she was not alone. A figure was standing in the corner, its dark eyes like blots of ink in a parchment face. It was dressed in a grey woollen gown, and its hair was drawn back into a severe chignon. It was holding a taper, and there was a sepulchral look about it. She wondered if one of the other servants had played a trick on her by putting a mannequin in her room to frighten her ... until it suddenly moved, and Helena realized with a creeping sensation that it was not a mannequin, but a woman of flesh and blood.

The woman ignored Helena and used the taper to light the candles. The gesture seemed territorial, as though she was saying to Helena, *This is my room, and you do not belong here.*

'I thought you would like a fire,' said the woman at last, putting down the taper. Her words were welcoming, but her voice was hollow and it sent a chill down Helena's back. 'The day is very cold.'

'Yes, it is,' said Helena, having a sudden urge to flee.

'You have had a long journey?' the woman asked.

'I have been travelling all day.'

'You are very young to be a housekeeper,' said the woman.

Helena hesitated. Until she knew to whom she was speaking, she did not know what tone to take. Was this a member of the family? A distant relative of Lord Torkrow, perhaps? Or another servant?

'Perhaps,' she said cautiously. 'And you are?'

'Miss Parkins.'

So this was Miss Parkins, the servant his lordship trusted absolutely. They made a fine pair, she thought. They were both intimidating in different ways.

'His lordship mentioned you,' said Helena. 'I am not sure what your position is?'

'My *position*,' said Miss Parkins, allowing the word to pass her lips as though it was a spider, 'is unusual. I came here many years ago as a lady's maid. Now, I help his lordship in whatever capacity he desires.'

Helena gave a tentative smile, wondering if it was possible to make a friend of the woman, for if she had been at the castle for a long time she must have known her aunt.

'You must have been a great help to the previous housekeeper,' she said.

28

The woman said nothing. There was something unsettling about her, beyond her appearance, and as Helena looked at her she began to realize that the face had no expression. When the woman spoke, she did not smile, or frown, or look surprised. She seemed, as she had seemed at first sight, like a waxwork dummy. 'It must have been difficult for you when she left. She left very quickly,' said Helena, persevering.

'She did.'

'Her sister was ill, I understand? It must have been inconvenient for his lordship to have her leave so suddenly. Was her sister very ill? Could she not have given him some warning?'

'Servants these days care for no one but themselves,' said Miss Parkins in a toneless voice.

Helena felt a retort spring to her lips, but she was prevented from uttering it by a flicker of interest in Miss Parkins's eyes. She sensed a strong and malevolent personality at work behind the maid's immobile face, and realized she could not afford to make any mistakes, so she stifled her retort, and said, 'It was very good of you to light a fire for me; it's cheerful to see the flames. It was very cold on the moor, and the castle is not much warmer.'

29

'The scullery maid will do it for you in future,' said Miss Parkins.

'Then you do not usually . . . ?' asked Helena, trailing off as she saw a gleam of sour amusement in Miss Parkins's eye.

'Light fires for the housekeeper? No, I do not.'

'It was good of you to do it on this occasion.' As Miss Parkins showed no signs of leaving, Helena said, in a friendly manner, 'If you do not mind, I am very tired. I have had a long journey, and if I am to be capable of fulfilling my duties tomorrow, I must get some rest.'

'As you wish,' said Miss Parkins.

But although she had accepted her dismissal, Helena was under no illusions: it was Miss Parkins who held the power, Miss Parkins who had agreed to leave, and not Helena who had dismissed her.

As Miss Parkins left the room, she left a chill in the air and Helena crossed to the door, on an impulse pulling a chair against it.

She went over to the fire and held her hands out to feel the heat. Aunt Hester had never mentioned Miss Parkins, and yet she must have known her.

Helena stared into the fire, as though she would be able to see her aunt in the flames.

Aunt Hester, she thought, why did you leave? Where did you go? Why did you not write to tell me you were leaving? And why did you lie to Lord Torkrow, telling him you needed to tend your sick sister, when I am your only relative?

* ★ ★ ★

Simon, Lord Torkrow, stood by the window in the library, looking out over the courtyard. It was too dark to see anything but the silhouette of the outer wall in the distance, with a patch of grey where the archway cut through it, and beyond, the deep dark of the moor.

He turned round as the door opened and Miss Parkins entered the room. She had not knocked, or waited for permission to enter. She stood before him in a respectful attitude, but her face was devoid of all emotion. Her dark eyes looked out from her white face, their large pupils seeming to swallow the light, but as she looked at him, he wondered what was going on behind them. Her black hair was pulled back into a bun, and he thought, with a passing fascination, that in all the years he had known her, he had never seen her hair loose. He did not know how old she was.

She had a quality of stillness about her that made her seem scarcely alive. That had not always been the case. There had been a time when she had been vital.

'There is a woman here,' she said.

'Yes, I know. She is the new housekeeper.'

'Is she?'

'What do you mean?' he asked sharply.

'She is very young for such a position.'

'It is not easy to get servants these days, particularly in such a remote corner.'

'She is not wearing a wedding band,' said Miss Parkins.

'It is possible she calls herself Mrs for reasons of employment, or that she has had to sell her wedding ring,' he said.

Inwardly, however, he berated himself, for he had not noticed her lack of a ring, and had been too ready to accept her as the person she claimed to be.

'Perhaps.'

'I will call in at the registry office the next time I am in York,' he said. 'Someone there will have met Elizabeth Reynolds and I can find out what she looks like, and see if her description matches this young woman.'

'Have you questioned her about her previous employment?'

'Yes.'

'A pity. If you had been on your guard, you

might have laid a trap for her.'

'What's done is done, but we must be careful. Watch her, Parkins. See where she goes, and what she does. Make yourself her shadow. Find out if she knows how to keep house. Because if she is not who she claims to be, then we must be prepared.'

'And if she discovers what has happened here?'

'She must be stopped.'

She looked at him unwaveringly.

'Very good, *my lord*.'

There was an almost imperceptible note of scorn in her voice when she said *my lord*, and it did not escape him.

You don't think I should be the earl, he thought. You think the title should belong to another.

'Very well, Parkins. You are dismissed.'

She did not blink. She did not speak. But when he addressed her as the servant she was, he could feel the venom coming from her.

She unfolded her hands and moved to the door, going through it in a gliding action, and leaving the room on noiseless feet.

He knew what she felt about him. He knew that she blamed him, that she had always blamed him.

Perhaps she was right.

33

Helena unpacked her few belongings, hanging her two woollen gowns in the wardrobe, and putting her chemise and petticoat in the top drawer, together with her handkerchiefs and her woollen stockings. Her shoes she put next to the bed. Then she took the hot brick from its place by the fire and put it between the sheets.

It was not the first night she had been expecting. She had been hoping for a warm welcome from her aunt, and after their reunion she had been intending to tell her of Mr Gradwell's proposal, and to hear her aunt's advice.

Caroline had been in no doubt. 'Marry him, Helena,' she had said. 'He's a kind man, a gentleman. He'll take care of you. You'll have servants of your own, instead of having to be a servant. You'll never have to sleep in an attic again.'

But Helena was still uncertain. She wanted a home of her own, yes, and it would be good to be no longer at someone else's beck and call, but she was not sure she could face a future with Mr Gradwell. He had kissed her once, and although the experience had not been unpleasant, she had hoped for something more.

Where heart, and soul, and sense, in concert move . . .
Each kiss a heart-quake . . . .

Each kiss a heart-quake, she thought with longing. There had been no quaking of her heart when Mr Gradwell kissed her. But was Byron's poetry a true vision of love? Or was it simply a romantic dream?

What would it really be like, to be married? she wondered, as she brushed her hair; to live with a man every day, to share a home with him, and to be with him every day of her life?

Aunt Hester knew. Aunt Hester had been married to Uncle George, and could tell her what to expect, as well as helping her to decide whether or not she could be happy in a marriage to Mr Gradwell. But Aunt Hester had disappeared.

She undressed in front of the fire, stepping out of her gown and stripping off her underwear before lifting her nightgown over her head. As she did so, she caught sight of her hand and she froze. She was not wearing a wedding ring. She should have thought of it sooner, but it was too late to do anything about it now. Besides, Lord Torkrow seemed to have accepted her. He knew as well as she did that many women had become destitute after losing their husbands at Waterloo, and had been forced to sell their jewellery in order to stay alive.

She climbed into bed. The hot brick had warmed the sheets, and she pushed it further down the bed, resting her toes on it and basking in its heat. She blew out her candle then, worn out from her day, she fell asleep.

★　★　★

It seemed hardly any time before she awoke to the sound of scratching on her door. At first she did not know where she was. The bed felt strange, and the red hangings confused her, but then it came back to her, and she remembered that she was in the castle. Fumbling on the table next to her bed she found the tinderbox and lit her candle then, throwing a wrapper round her shoulders, she removed the chair she had set in front of the door before calling, 'Come in.'

The door opened and Effie stood there. She wore a shapeless dress, over which was a large, grubby apron. In one hand she carried a jug of water from which steam was rising, and in the other she carried a bucket of coal.

'Good morning,' said Helena.

The girl made a nervous noise that could have been 'Morning', and then hurried across the room lumpishly, without grace. As Helena watched her, she thought of her aunt's letters, and as she recalled that Aunt Hester had taken a motherly interest in the girl, she hoped she might learn something from her.

Effie went over to the washstand and deposited the jug of water there clumsily, spilling the water.

'Oh, mum, I'm sorry, mum, I'm sorry,' said Effie, mopping up the water nervously with her apron.

'That's all right. You did not mean to do it,' said Helena.

'No, mum.'

The girl left the water half mopped and crossed to the grate, putting the bucket of coal down with a clatter that made Helena start, and then knelt down in front of the fire. Her skirt rode up to reveal a few inches of leg, and Helena saw that she had holes in her woollen stockings, which had been badly darned.

Effie picked up the poker, setting the other fire irons jangling, and began to rake the coals, which had turned to ash as the fire had burnt down overnight. The poker made a scraping noise across the iron grate, and there was a soft, shifting sound as the ash fell through into the box beneath.

'It's an early start for you,' said Helena, trying to put the girl at ease.

Effie dropped the poker with a clatter.

'Sorry, mum, I didn't mean to do it, I didn't mean to,' she said, grabbing at the poker.

'It's all right,' said Helena, wondering how many more times she was going to have to soothe the girl. You knew my aunt, she longed to say, but instead she went on, 'It must be confusing for you to have a new housekeeper in the castle. Perhaps you did not expect to find me still in bed. I am usually awake early, but I had a tiring day yesterday. Mrs Carlisle, my predecessor, was an early riser, I suppose?' she enquired casually.

'Yes, mum. Always up early she was. 'There's no use lying abed when there's work to be done', she used to say.'

'Quite right, too. There is plenty to do in the castle. You must be busy all day long.'

'Yes, mum. There's fires to be lit and there's that many steps, it's 'ard work.'

'Mrs Carlisle must have been sorry to leave the castle. She took a pride in her job, I believe.'

'Very particular, Mrs Carlisle was. The flowers 'ad to be fresh in summer. Very particular about 'er flowers, was Mrs Carlisle. I mustn't move anything on 'er desk, and I mustn't go through the drawers.'

'Did you used to go through the drawers?'

Helena asked in surprise.

Effie dropped the poker.

'I were only looking for some string,' she said, but she seemed nervous, and Helena wondered if she was speaking the truth. 'My stockings were falling down. Mrs Carlisle said I needed garters, she showed me 'ow to make 'em.'

'Of course,' said Helena. 'Did you find anything interesting when you were looking for the string?' she asked nonchalantly.

'Very particular about her pens, she was. Mended 'em 'erself. Didn't want no one touching her pens,' said Effie obliquely, picking up the poker and hanging it back on its stand, then she took a piece of newspaper from the top of the bucket of coals and crumpling it vigorously before laying it in the grate.

Helena's eyes were drawn to the girl's hands. They were large and strong and, as they picked up another piece of newspaper and crushed it, Helena found herself wondering what else the girl's hands could crush.

Changing the subject, she said, 'It must have been a shock to you when Mrs Carlisle left so suddenly.'

'I didn't know she was going,' said Effie. 'She said nothing to me, just went. One day she was here and the next day she wasn't.'

'Do you know why she had to leave?' Helena asked.

Effie sat back on her heels and rolled up a sheet of newspaper, winding it round her hand and knotting it before laying it on top of the crumpled paper.

'Do you?' asked Helena patiently.

Effie glanced over her shoulder and seemed reluctant to speak.

'I believe her sister was ill?' Helena prompted her.

'That's what he said.'

Helena had the feeling she was concealing something.

'And did you believe him?'

'It's not my place, mum, if Master says it, then it must be true.'

'Ah, yes. Do you like him? The master?'

'I reckon.'

But the girl's open manner had disappeared, and once she had finished lighting the fire she wiped her hands on her blackstreaked apron, then picking up the bucket she left the room.

Helena was left with much to think about. As she removed her nightgown and washed in the hot water, she thought that Effie had not told her everything she knew. But, if she stayed at the castle an extra day, there would be another morning, and another conversation whilst Effie lit the fire.

She dressed quickly, glad of her thick woollen gown and woollen stockings, brushed her hair and fastened it into a neat chignon, then, picking up her candle, she went down to the kitchen, following the route she had used on the previous day. As she went through the door into the servants' quarters, she once again had the unnerving feeling that she was being followed, but when she turned round, there was no one there.

She quickened her step, and was relieved to gain the sanctuary of the kitchen, where she found Mrs Beal baking bread. The smell of it filled the room and made Helena realize how hungry she was.

'Effie, set the kettle over the fire,' she said. Then, to Helena, she said, 'You'll have some rolls? They're freshly baked.'

Helena looked at the newly baked rolls that were set on the dresser, laid out on a clean cloth. With their golden tops, they looked appetizing.

'Yes, please.'

Mrs Beal set jars of home-made jam and honey on a table in the corner of the kitchen, and put out cups, saucers and plates. She added a mound of freshly churned butter to the table, and a jar of frothing milk. Soon a bowl of sugar and a pot of tea joined the rest.

'I'm ready for a bit of something myself,' said Mrs Beal.

'I see you have finished the fires,' said Helena to Effie, hoping to reassure the girl, so that the next time they met, she would be agreeable to talking.

Mrs Beal answered for her.

'Yes, she does the fires in the mornings, but his lordship doesn't want anyone in the library except the housekeeper and Miss Parkins, so she left a bucket of coal outside, as she always does. His lordship's told you you're to keep the library clean yourself?'

'Yes, he has. Miss Parkins does not see to it, then?'

'Miss Parkins doesn't see to a lot, from what I can see.'

'I am not quite sure what Miss Parkins's position is in the castle,' said Helena, gently probing, as Mrs Beal poured out the tea.

'That makes two of us,' said Mrs Beal. 'I wouldn't have much to do with her, if I were you. She comes down here from time to time, but I won't have anyone interfering in my kitchen. She looks at you sometimes . . . well, I've said enough.'

As Helena ate her rolls and drank her tea, the conversation turned to the idleness of dairy maids and the impossibility of running the kitchen adequately without any kitchen maids.

'In the old days, there were seven people working in the kitchen: Mrs Barnstaple the cook, me as her assistant, three kitchen maids and two scullery maids. Mind, we had a castle full of people to feed. His lordship and Master Richard . . . ' She tailed away, then finished, 'We'll not see those days back again.'

Helena tried to encourage her to say more, being sure there had been something important left unsaid, but Mrs Beal would not be drawn.

'Thank you for breakfast,' said Helena, when she had finished her meal. 'And now, I had better see to his lordship's fire.'

Taking up her candle, she left the kitchen, and then the servants' quarters, behind her, and emerged into the hall. A faint grey light could be seen coming through the windows. Outside, the sun was rising and it would soon be daylight.

She found the bucket of coal outside the library. Picking it up, she went in, but she was taken aback to see Lord Torkrow sitting behind the desk, looking at some papers. She had not expected him to rise so early, and she wished she had knocked.

He looked up as she stood there in the

doorway. As she felt his eyes run over her, she was conscious of a sudden unease, and again she wondered if he had been fooled by her deception, or if he knew that she was not who she claimed to be. She told herself there was no way he would know, but even so she felt anxious, for there was something about the way he looked at her . . .

'I'm sorry,' she said. 'I thought the room was empty.'

'You may see to the fire,' he replied.

She walked across the room, conscious of his eyes on her, and then poured coal on to the small flames.

'Tell me, how do you find the castle, now that you have had an opportunity to see it in daylight?' he said.

She was surprised by his question, for it was not the sort of thing that most earls would ask their servants. She replied, 'I find it . . . interesting.'

'You do not find it too remote?' he queried.

'No, my lord.'

'That is surprising. Most people are disinclined to work in such an isolated spot. It preys on their nerves. The loneliness becomes oppressive. After a time, they find themselves imagining things.'

There seemed to be something behind his words. Was he warning her about something, or was he trying to find out if she had heard anything unusual?

'I have no difficulty in working here,' she said.

'Perhaps you are used to the moors?'

'I have never seen them before. I think they are beautiful,' she added.

'You think so? I used to think so, once.' His voice dropped and his eyes fell to the desk. He was not seeing the desk, thought Helena, he was seeing something far away, and she wondered why he no longer liked his surroundings. He roused himself. 'If you are not used to the moors, then you perhaps grew up in gentler climes?'

'Yes, my lord. I grew up by the sea, in Cornwall,' she told him.

His eyes narrowed. 'You do not speak with a Cornish accent,' he remarked.

'I left Cornwall many years ago, when I was fifteen.'

'Ah, I see. Then why did you leave?'

'My father died, and my mother took me to live in Manchester . . . ' She trailed away, suddenly conscious of the fact that Mrs Reynolds might have mentioned her abode. She felt herself colouring and hoped he would not notice, or that he would put her sudden flush down to the heat of the fire, but instead she was disturbed to see him turning questioning eyes towards her, as if to say, *Now what were you about to tell me?* She began to think that his questions were more than a passing curiosity in a new servant; they were designed to find out if she was really Mrs Reynolds.

'And do you like Manchester?' he asked.

'It is my home,' she said, 'but no, I do not like it.'

'I am surprised. You are young. I thought you would enjoy the liveliness of a city. It must seem very quiet here by comparison.'

'It seems peaceful,' she said. 'I like the quiet.'

'And when did you go into service?' he asked, returning to his earlier theme.

She was about to say, 'A year ago,' when she realized that Mrs Reynolds had been in service for far longer.

'Well?' he asked.

'I cannot recall exactly.'

There was a silence. Then he said, 'In your letter, you stated that you had been a housekeeper for three years.' He shot her a sudden glance, and said, 'You do not have the look of a servant.'

She felt her heart beating more quickly.

'My father was a gentleman,' she said, 'and I was raised to be a lady. But he fell on hard times and our circumstances changed, so I

46

had no choice but to earn a living.'

He said nothing, and she wondered what was going through his mind. Unwillingly, Helena found herself remembering some of the things her aunt had said about the man in front of her. *Afraid of him in the village, they are. The stories they tell! It's always the same in these remote places, but I've seen nothing amiss. He's not an easy master, but I'll say this for him, he's fair.*

She only hoped her aunt had been right.

At last he said, 'And now you are keeping house in a castle. Not many people wish to work in such a large establishment, especially with so few servants. What is your opinion of the castle, now that you have seen it?'

She looked round the large room.

'I think it has been neglected, but it is a beautiful building, and with hard work, I think it will be possible to bring it back to life.'

'You are an optimist, I see. Hard work will go some way to making it brighter, but hard work has its limits and will not remove the draughts.'

'Large fires and carefully placed screens can do much to limit their effect,' she said thoughtfully, wondering how best the disadvantages of such an old building could be overcome.

'There is no money to waste on large fires at Stormcrow.'

He appeared to become lost in his thoughts, and she said no more.

He roused himself.

'Very well. The fire will do now. You may return to your duties.'

'Very good, my lord.'

Helena left the room, relieved that she had escaped unscathed, and made her way to the housekeeper's room, where she hoped she might find a letter or a diary entry, perhaps, that would tell her something about her aunt's decision to leave the castle, and her intended destination.

3

As she opened the door, she breathed in the scent of lavender, and it awakened memories in her. She remembered how, as a little girl, she had helped her aunt to pick flowers and herbs, and how her aunt had showed her how to plait lavender. Her aunt had always had a plait of it attached to her belt. She remembered summer holidays when her father had been alive, and, in her mind's eye, she saw her mother and Aunt Hester cutting flowers and herbs, whilst she and her father sat on a rug beneath the chestnut tree with their books. She could remember the pulled thread on the rug, and she could feel its softness beneath her fingers.

She went in, thinking how lucky Aunt Hester was to have such an attractive room to work in. It was newly decorated in cheerful colours, with flowered wall hangings echoing the gold damask of the sofa. There were vases on the console tables, and although they were empty, they were still decorative.

Diamond-paned windows looked out on to the side of the castle. It was a bleak prospect at present, but under a summer sky it would be attractive. Her own position as a housekeeper had not been so grand, and her room had been a dingy room at the back of the house, with a window looking on to a brick wall. She had almost been glad to leave it when the Hamiltons had moved to Wales — almost, but not quite, as she had needed the position, and without it she had been reduced to sharing a room with Caroline.

She went over to the hearth, where there was a fire burning in the grate, noticing that the shelves had been dusted and the furniture polished. She set down the coal bucket and then let her eyes wander over the chintz sofa set beneath the window and the matching chair that was placed by the fire. There were two console tables, one by the chair and one by the sofa, and in the middle of the room was a desk. She went over to the desk, which had a number of pigeon holes down the side and across the top. On the desk was a large book, an inkstand, and a shaker of sand. In front of it was an inlaid chair.

Helena sat down and opened the book. It was in the form of a diary, but it held nothing useful, simply details of the work that needed to be done around the castle. The notes stopped just over three weeks before.

She turned her attention to the pigeon holes, but they revealed nothing more than sample menus, letters to and from tradesmen, and other household items. Then she opened the first drawer.

What did Effie find when she looked for some string? Helena wondered.

But a search of the drawers found nothing more than some household documents, some paper, a quill pen and a large bunch of keys, which she took out and fastened to her belt. There was nothing more of interest.

So what did Effie see? she asked herself. Why did it upset her? And where had it gone? Unless Effie had seen nothing, and had simply been nervous because she had let slip that she had been guilty of going through the housekeeper's desk.

As Helena looked round the room she began to think that this must be the case. The chintz upholstery and the placid ticking of the clock were reassuring. Their very ordinariness reminded her that her aunt had been an ordinary woman, and that there must be an ordinary reason for her disappearance.

Maybe she did, indeed, have a sister, thought Helena, or perhaps, a half sister she had never mentioned. Maybe there was a reason for Aunt Hester not mentioning her. Perhaps they had been estranged.

Perhaps Aunt Hester wrote to me, she thought, but perhaps the letter was lost in the post, or perhaps my aunt gave it to the footman to post, and he forgot about it.

The more she thought about it, the more likely it seemed. There were very few servants in the castle, and with no one to keep them to their tasks, something like posting a letter could easily be overlooked.

She saw a row of bells on the wall by the fireplace, and rang the one labelled 'Footman'. Soon afterwards the footman entered the room. He was wearing livery, but some of the braid was missing from his coat, and the buttons were dull. His person reflected the same carelessness: his hair had been combed, but a tuft stuck up at the back, and his nails were dirty.

He stood in front of her with a strange expression. It was part insolence and part insinuation, and there was a sly look on his face. He rubbed his hands together in an unpleasant manner and looked at her from the corner of his eye, as though he was sizing her up.

She wondered if he had looked that way at her aunt, or if he was simply doing it to her because of her youth.

'Your name?' she asked him, injecting a note of authority into her voice: if he thought he could patronize her, he would soon learn his mistake. She had dealt with difficult footmen before, and would most probably have to do so again.

'Dawkins, missus,' he said.

'Dawkins. I have summoned you here to ask you how Mrs Carlisle went about sending her letters. I will have my own letters to send, and I need to know the routine at the castle. Do I leave them on my desk when they are ready to go?'

'I don't come in the housekeeper's room, not unless I'm sent for,' he said.

There was something self-consciously virtuous about his reply, and Helena found herself thinking that he probably did enter the housekeeper's room uninvited, though what he could want there she could not imagine, unless it was to snoop through the desk, in order to see if there was anything of use to him.

'What am I to do with my letters, then?' she asked.

'You have to leave them in the hall. There's a pewter bowl on a table under the window at the far end, in between two suits of armour. His lordship franks them, then I takes them to the village.'

'I see. And when do they go? Every week? Every day?'

'Whenever his lordship sees fit,' he said.

'And what happens to the letters until

then? Do they remain in the bowl?'

'Nowhere else for them to go,' he said with an insolent grin.

Helena felt herself bridling.

'Did that suit Mrs Carlisle?' she asked.

'What d'you mean?'

'I mean, did she ever ask you to take one of her letters, even if his lordship had no letters to send? Perhaps she had something that needed to go urgently, and could not wait.'

'What kind of thing?' he asked craftily.

'I have no idea,' said Helena quellingly. 'Anything that might need to be sent in a hurry, and might perhaps require a speedy answer.'

'No, missus, there were nothing like that.'

'Did she send letters often, then?'

A sly look crept into his eye, and Helena was sure he knew something she didn't. It seemed he could say more if he wanted to.

'No, missus. Once a week, as a general rule. She weren't a great letter writer.'

'I see.' She paused, to give him a chance to say more, but he remained silent. 'Very well, thank you, Dawkins.'

'Thank you, missus. Will that be all?'

'No. Not quite. I need to find out a little more about the castle, to help me with my duties. Tell me, what other servants work here? There is a butler, I suppose? And his lordship must have a valet.'

'There's no butler. The last one died, and his lordship never replaced him. And his lordship's valet left when . . . he don't have a valet any more. He likes to see to himself. There's not many as'll work in the castle. Servants are hard to come by.'

He puffed his chest out, and she realized that he was taunting her, daring her to interfere with him, and warning her that, if she did, he might decide not to work there either.

'Then what other servants are there in the castle besides you, Mrs Beal, Effie and Miss Parkins?'

'There ain't no more.'

'None? How did Mrs Carlisle keep the castle clean without any maids to help her?'

'It weren't always that way. There were two maids here when Mrs Carlisle worked here. Sally and Martha, they were. But they wouldn't stay in the castle.'

'Oh? Why not?' asked Helena, wondering if he would tell her more than Mrs Beal had done.

'It was the stories, missus. About his lordship.'

Helena felt her pulse quicken, but she gave no sign of it.

'What kind of stories?' she asked.

'People likes to talk in a village,' he said. 'There's always been things said about the Stormcrows.'

'A lot of nonsense, I expect,' said Helena encouragingly.

He gave another sly smile.

'You, at least, do not seem to believe them, or you would not still be working here,' she said, hoping to coax him into saying something further.

'Oh, I'm safe enough. Nothing'll happen to me. There's never anything happened to a man,' he said.

He was toying with her, trying to unsettle her.

'I'm glad to hear it. But surely there hasn't been anything happening to women, either?' she asked.

He said nothing.

'Why did the maids leave?' she prompted him.

'It were on account of Mrs Carlisle,' he said, his desire to talk overcoming his desire to have her in his power. 'Disappeared in the dead of night, she did, and Sally said she heard crying from the east wing, up in the attic, and the following day, Martha said she heard it, too. 'It's a cat', I said to them, but they wouldn't listen. Gave in their notice and went home.'

Helena felt a shiver run up her spine.

'Did you find it?' she asked. 'The cat?'

'Didn't need to. The crying stopped, so it must have got out. But it's better not to go near the attics, all the same.'

'Oh? Why?' she asked.

'Rotting floorboards, missus. Dangerous, they are. Could give way at any minute. Anyone who goes up there could go crashing right through and break their necks.'

He gave her an insolent look, and the thought flashed through her mind that she would not like to be alone with Dawkins in the attic.

She questioned him further about his fellow servants, but he had nothing to say, other than that Mrs Beal was a good cook and that Effie was a clumsy thing.

'And Miss Parkins?' asked Helena.

He hesitated, and she thought: He is afraid of Miss Parkins, too.

When he had told her all he could, she dismissed him.

Once he had left the room, she took her letter out of her pocket. She had not been going to send it, thinking that she would see Caroline soon, but she changed her mind. She wanted to see if a letter sent from the castle would arrive. If it never reached its destination, then it was possible that Aunt

Hester had written to her, but that Aunt Hester's letter had never reached its destination, either.

Finding sealing wax in the drawer, she was about to apply it to her letter when she paused. If Dawkins read it — and having met him, she would not put it past him — she did not want him to discover that she was not Mrs Reynolds. She found paper and a quill, and she rewrote the letter. As she began to write, she was pleased with the pen's smoothness, and was reminded of Aunt Hester, who had prided herself on her quills. She had told Helena on more than one occasion that she could not hope to write a neat hand with an ill-mended pen, advice that had gone home, for Helena had always admired her aunt's handwriting.

She thought for a few minutes, composing the letter carefully in her head, and then began to write.

My dearest Caroline,
    I have arrived at the castle, and his lordship has given me the position as his new housekeeper. I have not found what I was looking for, but I have not despaired of finding it either, and mean to persevere. I am sure you will be pleased to know that I am well. You will not have time to write

me more than a line or two, I don't
suppose, but let me know if you are well,
and if you hear anything of H, please let
me know. You may send your reply to me
here at the castle. Address it to:
  Mrs Reynolds
  Torkrow Castle
  Seremoor
  Yorkshire
  Fondest regards,
  Your dear friend

She scrawled an illegible signature at the
bottom of the letter, then sanded it, and,
when it had dried, she folded it and fastened
it with sealing wax, and then she went out
into the hall, and looked about her for the
table.

Seen in full daylight, the hall was even
larger than she had imagined, and just as
austere. The light glinted on the silver armour
and lit the stone with a cold light.

Her eye fell on the oak table, and she
crossed to it and put her letter in the bowl.
There were no further letters there, and she
wondered how long it would be before it was
sent.

She heard a clanking sound and started,
but, turning round, she saw that it was only
Effie, carrying a bucket of coal towards the

housekeeper's room. As she watched her, Helena thought that, although the girl was young and nervous, if she was capable of going through the housekeeper's desk, she might also be capable of tampering with the mail. Perhaps she had interfered with it innocently, dropping the bowl as she dusted beneath it, and seeing that a letter was damaged, perhaps she had taken it in order to escape a scolding. It was possible. She questioned the girl gently, but Effie maintained that she never touched the mail, so she let her go about her business.

Who else crossed the hall in the course of the day? she wondered, as she glanced at her letter, which lay defenceless in the bowl. Mrs Beal might venture into the hall occasionally, but Helena did not believe Mrs Beal would interfere with the post. And then there was Miss Parkins. Helena shivered as she thought of the waxen face and the long, cold hands. Miss Parkins would be capable of taking one of Aunt Hester's letters, but why?

There was no one else . . . except Martha and Sally. They had both been at the castle when her aunt had been there, and perhaps one of them had seen it, or taken it.

There was a sound of footsteps behind her, and his lordship came into view, followed by Dawkins, who was hurrying to keep up.

'Go to the stables. Tell them to ready my horse. I want it brought round to the front of the castle.'

'Yes, my lord, very good, my lord,' said Dawkins, bowing, before heading towards the door.

Summoning her courage, Helena spoke to the earl as he passed.

'Might I speak to you, my lord?' she asked.

He turned towards her, and she wondered what he was thinking. Nothing very pleasant, if his expression was any guide. His mouth was grim, and his deep-set eyes looked haggard.

'Well?' he demanded.

'It is about the maids, my lord. I understand there used to be some working here. I do not believe I can keep the castle clean without help. There is a great deal of dusting and polishing to be done, to say nothing of the floors to be washed. Mrs Carlisle had some housemaids to help her, I understand.'

He looked at her as though weighing his words and then said, 'And so you would like me to appoint some?'

'I could take care of that, my lord, if I had permission to employ, perhaps, two girls.'

'Very well. You may walk in to the village on Friday. See to it, Mrs Reynolds, but don't disturb me with this matter again.'

'Very good, my lord.'

He strode past her, and went into the library.

Perhaps Martha and Sally could shed new light on her aunt's sudden departure, she thought . . . and perhaps they could tell her more about the crying in the attic.

For some reason the tale had disturbed her. It had only been the sound of a cat . . . and even if it had, by an chance, been a human being, it would not have been Aunt Hester. Helena could not remember Aunt Hester ever crying.

But a small voice asked her: what if it had been Aunt Hester? What if Aunt Hester had had some bad news, and had left the castle accordingly?

She found that she was walking towards the stairs, almost without her own volition, and she knew she would have no peace until she had been to the attic, to see if, perhaps, there might be any evidence that her aunt had been there, and now was a good time, for there was no chance of encountering Dawkins, who was on an errand for Lord Torkrow.

Lifting the hem of her skirt, she mounted the stairs, going up to the second floor and then looking for the steps that led to the attic. She found them at last, tucked away on a corner, a narrow spiral staircase, lit by arrow slits in the walls.

She went up as fast as she safely could, and finally reached the top. To her left was a row of windows, and from them she could see the moors stretching out before her, their undulating hills and hummocks a dull green against the grey sky. Set in their midst, the castle was isolated and cut off, and she was forcefully reminded of the fact that it was a long way back to town, and civilization. Anything could happen in the castle, and no one would ever know . . .

She turned her attention back to the task in hand. She saw a long corridor on either side of her, from which various doors opened off. At the end of each corridor was a heavy oak door, the doors to the east and west wings, she supposed.

Dawkins had said the crying came from the east wing, and, glancing at the dim sun that shone weakly through a rent in the clouds to get her bearings, she chose the east door. She tried to open it, but it was locked.

She began to try the keys. One by one, she tried them all, but none of them fitted. She listened at the door, but could hear nothing, so she knocked on the door, and called out, but there was no reply.

There is no one there, she thought. The

attic is disused. The crying was nothing more than a cat, and the animal escaped weeks ago.

But a need to get into the east wing and see for herself had taken hold of her, and she went into the large attic room that was nearest to the east wing, hoping that there might be a way through. It was a vast space, and draughts swirled around her. It was full of old pieces of furniture, a selection of childhood toys and assorted broken chairs, tables and household objects. The floorboards were bare. She went into the corners, but there was no sign of a door, or a way into the east wing, and reluctantly she had to admit defeat.

She went out on to the landing and a movement below caught her eye. Through the window she saw a solitary figure in the courtyard below: Lord Torkrow. Where was he going? she wondered.

As he headed towards his horse, he stopped suddenly, and she felt an unaccountable sense of alarm. She shrank back as he looked up, and his eyes raked the window. As her heart began to race, she wondered why she was so afraid. She had every right to be in the attic. But even so, she felt a sense of relief when she heard the horse's hoofs on the gravel and knew he was on his way.

4

Helena was relieved to join Mrs Beal in the kitchen again for dinner. After an unsettling day, here, with cheerful company, the castle seemed less menacing, and Helena felt her confidence returning. She knew she needed to be careful of what she said, but she was not as frightened of making a slip in front of Mrs Beal as she had been in front of Lord Torkrow, because Mrs Beal would probably not notice. And if she did, she would probably forget it the moment a pie needed taking out of the oven.

'Yes, you'll need some maids,' said Mrs Beal, as the two sat down to a nourishing meal of chicken and potatoes, and Helena told her that she had spoken to the earl. 'There's no way you can run the castle without them. It's a long walk to the village across the moor, mind, so make sure you're wrapped up warm, and mind you wear stout shoes.'

'I will,' said Helena.

'Go and see the rector's wife, Mrs Willis. She's used to finding maids for the castle. The last two left, silly girls. Said they'd heard a ghost, or some such nonsense. But work's scarce hereabouts, and there'll be two more to take their place.'

'Do you think the same two could be persuaded to return?' asked Helena. 'They would know their business,' she explained, when Mrs Beal looked surprised.

Mrs Beal considered. 'Maybe. Their fathers will want them working, that's for sure. If it hadn't been for the fact there was no housekeeper at the castle, they'd have made the girls go back to work at once, ghosts or no. But there were those in the village who said it wasn't right for girls to be working at the castle with no one but his lordship here. I'm down in the kitchen all day long, and the villagers know it.'

'But they would consider Miss Parkins a suitable chaperon, surely?' asked Helena, voicing the concern that had been troubling her.

Mrs Beal pulled a face. 'There's not many that like Miss Parkins hereabouts. Why keep a lady's maid when there's no lady? That's what the gossips say.'

'They can't think . . . ?'

'Why, bless you no, there's none so crazed as that, but there are those who say she knows things about him, things that could harm him, and that's why he keeps her here. There are those who say he can't afford to turn her away.'

'Do you believe it?' Helena asked, putting down her cup.

'Not I. He's a good master. Some are forever finding fault: the food's too rich, the food's too plain, there's too much spent, there's too much waste … nothing but complaints with some people. But he never criticizes. I can make what I want, as long as the housekeeper agrees. It's a good place, and I mean to keep it.'

As they ate, Helena asked, 'Dawkins doesn't eat in the kitchen, then?'

'He has his meal earlier, at four o'clock, with Effie. It leaves him free to attend to his lordship when his lordship eats his meal.'

'Do you know where his lordship has gone?' asked Helena.

'He's gone to York, maybe, to see to business.'

'And do you know when he is likely to return?'

'He never says. It would be easier if he did. He'll expect a hot meal when he gets back. But there, it's not his place to think of my convenience, it's mine to think of his.'

They finished their meal, and Helena retired for the night. Her footsteps sounded ominously on the stone floor, pattering like a frightened animal scurrying for shelter, and she thought she detected the sound of footsteps following her. Her mind worked feverishly, trying to convince herself that any stray footfalls were merely echoes, but she quickened her step nonetheless. Then she stopped abruptly, trying to catch whoever was following her, but there was no extra footfall. The echo was nothing but her imagination, she told herself, and hurried on.

The flickering light of her candle cast strange shadows on the walls, and she jumped at the sound of a door creaking somewhere below. The castle seemed full of mysteries, and she longed for the safety of her room.

She began to run, hastening up the stairs and along the corridor . . . and then stopped. She quickly retreated into an open doorway as she saw Miss Parkins at the end of the corridor, standing just outside her room. The maid's hand was on the door knob.

Helena's thoughts began to race. Was Miss Parkins about to go into her room? Or had she already been inside?

She shrank back as she heard Miss Parkins coming towards her and, afraid of being discovered, she slipped into an empty room. She snuffed her candle, for a strange fear had gripped her, and it did not leave her until Miss Parkins had walked past.

She waited until she was sure Miss Parkins had gone before stepping out again. The corridor was dark, and she had to let her eyes adjust to the gloom before she could go on. She began to regret having snuffed her candle. Feeling the wall at her right with one hand, she continued down the corridor and fumbled with her door knob, then turned it and went in. The fire was glowing in the hearth, and she quickly lit her candle from the flames, then lit the other candles. She looked around, wondering if Miss Parkins had entered the room but she could see no signs of it. Nothing seemed to have been disturbed. But Helena was still not comfortable. If Miss Parkins had not entered the room, then Helena felt that she had been about to do so. She determined to lock her door every time she left her room in future. She wanted no more unwelcome visits.

★   ★   ★

Simon, Lord Torkrow, arrived in York and then made his way to the office that had sent him Mrs Reynolds. He went in.

'May I help you?' asked the man behind the desk.

'You supplied me with a housekeeper, a

Mrs Elizabeth Reynolds. I would like to speak to the person who interviewed her and recommended her for the post.'

'If I might have a name?' enquired the young man.

'Lord Torkrow.'

'I will apprise Mr Wantage of your visit,' said the young man, bobbing into an inner office and returning a minute later to usher him in.

'Lord Torkrow, this is a pleasant surprise — an honour, an unexpected honour. I hope all is well at the castle? Mrs Reynolds suits, I trust?'

'Did you interview her?' asked Simon, taking the seat that was offered to him.

'No, that was my colleague, Mr Brunson.'

'I would like to speak with him.'

'I am afraid he is not here, he was taken ill on Monday with a putrid sore throat, but if I may be of assistance?'

'You met Mrs Reynolds?'

'No, I did not. I read her references, however, and they appeared to be in order. We have recommended her for positions before, and she has always given satisfaction. I hope there is nothing wrong?'

'I would like to speak to Mr Brunson as soon as he is well enough. You will write to me, and let me know when he is fit to be seen.'

'Yes, my lord, of course, my lord.'

'Good.' He thought for a moment, and then said, 'Your boy in the outer office. He met Mrs Reynolds?'

'Alas no, my lord. He has only just joined us. His predecessor is sadly deceased.'

'I see. Very well. Inform me when I might speak to Mr Brunson.'

'Yes, my lord, very good, my lord.'

He took his leave, with Mr Wantage bowing him out of the office, then set about paying attention to business.

★　★　★

The following morning, Helena was awake early, and was already dressed when Effie entered the room. She wanted to question the girl, and find out what she had discovered in the drawer in the housekeeper's room.

'Good morning,' she said, when Effie entered the room.

Effie grunted a reply, and set about seeing to the fire.

'I wonder if you can help me,' she said. She considered asking a direct question, but suspected it would produce nothing but anxiety in the girl, as it had when she had questioned her about the mail, and so she decided to lead up to it in a roundabout manner.

'I would like to make an inventory of the drawers in the housekeeper's desk — that means making a list of everything that's inside them,' she explained, as Effie turned and looked at her blankly. 'I need to know which of the things belong to the castle, and which belong to Mrs Carlisle. She might want to claim her belongings when her sister is feeling better, and I do not want to use them by mistake.'

'No, missus.'

'Can you remember what you saw there when you looked for some string?'

Effie turned back to the fire hurriedly, knocking the fire irons over in the process. They fell with a clatter, and Effie jumped, picking them up nervously and trying to hang them back in place, with hands that shook so much she had to make several attempts before succeeding.

'Can you remember what there was?' Helena prompted her.

Effie shook her head.

'Was there, perhaps, some writing paper?'

Effie jumped.

'There was a letter, perhaps?'

Effie's mouth clamped together, and her hands shook as she raked the grate.

'Do you remember anything at all?' Helena asked.

Effie shook her head, and concentrated vigorously on her task.

It was clear she was going to get nothing from the girl, at least for the moment, so she complimented her on her ability to lay a clean fire. Her praise went some way towards relaxing Effie, who picked up the empty bucket and hurried out of the room.

One avenue of exploration had led nowhere, but she hoped she might have better luck with another, and after taking breakfast with Mrs Beal in the kitchen, she went out to the stables, for she had remembered something overnight: Mrs Beal had mentioned in an earlier conversation that the coachman had taken her aunt to Draycot to catch the stage.

The stables were situated behind the castle, and the block was well tended. The noise of horses snuffling came from the stalls, and a glossy chestnut head looked out.

The black carriage, which Helena had ridden in on her journey across the moor, was standing in the stable yard, and the coachman was polishing the brass lamps.

'Good morning,' she said.

He looked up briefly and acknowledged her presence, before returning to his work.

'I wanted to thank you for driving me across the moor on my arrival here,' said Helena.

'His lordship's orders,' said the coachman.

'Quite so. It was good of him to take me up. It is not every earl who would make room in his carriage for his housekeeper.'

He grunted a reply and went on with his work.

'He seems to be a good master to work for,' she said.

He grunted again.

'He set you to drive my predecessor to the nearest town, so that she could catch the stage coach a few weeks ago, I understand.'

'Aye.'

'It was a very kind thing for him to do. Poor lady, having to leave in such a hurry.'

'Ah.'

'And so late at night. Was it not difficult for you to harness the horses?' she asked. He looked at her as though he thought she was a half wit. 'I'm afraid I know very little about horses. I have never learnt to ride, and I have ridden in a carriage only once or twice. But don't horses sleep, as we do? Did you have to wake them? Or had they not yet gone to bed?'

'Horses work here, same as everyone else,' he said.

'Even late at night?'

'Whenever his lordship commands.'

'It must be difficult driving across the moor in the dark,' she said. 'I am surprised Mrs

Carlisle wanted to venture out in the middle of the night. Did she not think it would be better to wait until morning?'

'No.'

A horse snorted.

'Was there a stagecoach to take her on when you left her? I hope she did not have to wait in an isolated spot, all on her own.'

'I left her at the inn,' he said.

'What a distressing thing for her, to have to make such a long journey.'

She paused, hoping he would reply, but he was a taciturn individual, more used to dealing with horses than with people, and he said nothing, just continued with his work.

'Where do the stagecoaches go from here?' she asked.

'North. South,' he said.

'And west and east, I suppose,' she said in disappointment.

'Most ways,' he agreed

'That is very convenient.'

He did not reply and reluctantly she left the stable yard. She bent her footsteps towards the castle, but she was disinclined to go back inside. She feared she would be overcome by the oppressive atmosphere, and her lack of progress in discovering her aunt's whereabouts. Instead, she decided to take a walk. It was a bright morning. The air was fresh, and the sun was shining. There was even a little warmth in its rays.

She began to walk across the lawns that led to the outer wall. To her right the drive led through the arch and out on to the moor. Directly in front of her was a set of stone steps leading up to the top of the wall.

As she took the steps, she wondered if the coachman had really taken her aunt to Draycot, or if he had simply said so on Lord Torkrow's orders.

In the fresh air, with the solid feel of the stone steps beneath her, it was easy to dismiss such suspicions.

She reached the top of the wall. It was windy, and she pulled her cloak tightly round her. She looked out across the moors. The landscape looked gentler than it had done the previous day. The colours were brighter, and the air softer. Far off, she saw a gleam of yellow. The cheerful colour stood out against the muted greens of the moor, and she saw that a few early daffodils were in flower, nestling in a sheltered hollow.

She descended the steps and went out of the gate, making her way towards the bright flowers, which were nodding their heads in the breeze. She picked a bunch and then carried them back to the castle. Taking them into the flower room, she arranged them in a vase, and then carried them back to the housekeeper's room.

On the way she passed the library, and thinking that the fire might need mending, she went in. She put the vase on the mantelpiece whilst she poured more coal on the dying flames, then allowed herself a few minutes to look at the books that lined the walls. She had read a great deal as a child, but after her father's death there had been little money for books and she had purchased only two the previous year. But here was a feast of literature. There were works by Shakespeare, Marlowe, Chaucer and many more, some in fine covers, and some in books that were falling apart with age. She took down a copy of *Le Morte D'Arthur* and lost track of time as she became absorbed. She was lost to the world, but the sound of the door opening shocked her back to reality. She turned round to see Lord Torkrow standing in the doorway.

'I have just been repairing the fire,' she said, hastily putting the book back on the shelf.

He glanced round the room, and his eyes fell on the vase of flowers. She was about to hurry over to the mantelpiece when, to her surprise, his face relaxed. It was warmer and more open than before, and she felt a rush of some strange feeling rise up within her. She had not realized he could look so appealing.

'There haven't been daffodils in here since . . . ' he said.

There was such a wistful tone in his voice that she held her breath, wondering what he would say next, but he never finished the sentence. Instead, his voice trailed away, and Helena dare not move. He was lost in thought, going back to some previous time, and the memory seemed to please him. But it was made up of pain as well as pleasure, she thought, because there was a twist to his mouth that cut her to the quick. She was surprised at the stab of pain that shot through her, because she had not been prepared for it, and for a moment she saw him not as an enigmatic and forbidding figure, but as a man of flesh and blood.

What had hurt him? she wondered. Why did the simple sight of daffodils bring him pain?

He roused himself, and turning towards her, he said, 'You have done well.' He noticed that she was standing by the bookcase and said, 'You are interested in books?'

'Yes,' she said.

'Then you must use the library. You may choose something to read whenever you wish.'

For a moment there was a gleam of

friendship illuminating the room. It warmed her, as the unexpected gleam of daffodils had warmed the moor. It relaxed something deep inside her, something that had long been frozen, but in this strange place and stranger situation, it started to come to life.

'Thank you,' she said.

'You were looking at this?' he asked, going over to the shelf and taking out *Le Morte D'Arthur*, which she had not pushed far enough back on the shelf.

'Yes.'

'Then take it. I think you will enjoy it.'

He handed her the volume.

'It must have taken generations to assemble a library like this,' she said, looking round at the laden shelves as she took it.

'Yes, it did.'

A sense of longing welled up inside her. She had no home, and, saving her aunt, no family. She did not know where she would be in a year, or even a month's time. She would have to go where the wind blew her. But he belonged to the castle. He was lucky. He had his place in the world by right. She sometimes wondered, in the dead of night, if she would ever find hers.

'It must be a wonderful feeling, to have a home, to belong,' she said.

He looked at her strangely and she realized

that she had forgotten to whom she was speaking. The gleam of friendship he had shown her had lowered her defences and made her forget her position, so that she had spoken to him as an equal, but she quickly reminded herself that she and Lord Torkrow were not equals. They were master and servant, separated not only by rank but by deception and the disappearance of her aunt.

'I have work to do . . . ' she said.

She began to head towards the door, but, as she tried to pass him, he put out his arm, resting it on the desk so that he was blocking her path.

'You call it belonging,' he said. 'I call it being trapped.'

He looked down at her, and she felt herself being pulled into the strange aura that surrounded him, a magnetic strength that held her fast.

'The weight of the castle oppresses me,' he said, looking deep into her eyes as though seeking understanding. 'At night, the walls close in.'

'But it is your home,' she said, searching his eyes.

'It is not my home. It is my tomb.'

All light and warmth had gone from his voice, and she was once more afraid of him, but the fear was tempered with intrigue. She

80

clenched and unclenched her hands, then said, 'But you can leave the castle if you want to.'

'Can I?' he said with bitterness.

'You were returning to it on the day I arrived, so you must have left,' she said, striving to remain calm, 'and you left again yesterday.'

'Briefly, yes. But the castle keeps drawing me back. It is not fond of letting its inhabitants go.' He looked deep into her eyes once more, and his words sounded like a warning. 'One way or another, it finds a way to keep them.'

He fell silent, and Helena stood there, unable to pass, but unwilling to disturb him. He had become lost in thought, and his eyes were fixed on the floor. After a minute he roused himself.

'You must tell me what you think of the book when you have read it,' he said, dropping his arm so that she could pass. 'We are not unlike the knights of old, you and I. We, too, have monsters to fight.'

Helena quietly left the room. She went upstairs, taking her book into her bedroom. As she put it on the table, she wondered if her aunt had sat at that very table writing her letters, and wondered, if the table could talk, what tales it would tell?

* * *

Simon scarcely noticed the door closing. He was lost in his thoughts, seeing the past, when the castle had flourished. It had been full of noise and colour when his parents had been alive, until . . .

Strange how the sight of the daffodils had taken him back to that time, their bright yellow and green reminding him that there were colours beyond the stone, oak and metal of the castle.

How soft they had seemed, how fragile, as she had been soft and fragile . . .

But he must be on his guard, he must not lower his defences again.

* * *

It was evening. Having dined with Mrs Beal, Helena was sitting by the fire in her room. The curtains were drawn, shutting out the black night. She was leafing through *Le Morte D'Arthur*, looking at the illustrations, which were beautifully done. It was as she looked at a picture of a man with a candle that a thought struck her. In the absence of a key to the east wing of the attic, she might be able to find out if anyone was in there by going out into the grounds and seeing if there was a light in the window. It was still early, not yet seven o'clock, and she decided to go before it was too late.

She laid aside her book, uncurled herself from the chair and put on her cloak and heavy shoes. She tied her bonnet under her chin, pulled on her gloves then went down the stairs.

She slipped out of a side door, and walked across the lawn, which was silvered by the moon. She walked away from the castle, so that she could see the windows clearly when she looked back. When she felt she had gone far enough she turned and looked up, but they were dark. There was not a glimmer of light anywhere. She had been hoping to see something, but there was nothing.

She was just about to go back inside when she caught sight of a lantern bobbing along in the distance. Her senses were immediately alert. Who would be going out with a lantern at this time of night? And where were they going? She hesitated. A part of her wanted to ignore it, but curiosity won over caution, and she began to follow cautiously.

The light disappeared briefly and Helena realized that whoever had been carrying it had gone through the archway in the outer wall. She followed quickly, taking care to stay well back so that she would not be seen.

She passed through the arch and saw the light again, in the distance. It looked unearthly, bobbing along, detached from the ground, a ball of glowing yellow in the darkness. She followed it, but soon she began to grow uneasy as she felt the gravel give way to coarse grass and found herself walking across the moor.

The wind whipped round her, stronger than it had been in the courtyard, pulling her cloak open and knifing her with freezing air. She pulled it around her, holding it closed with folded arms, and went on.

An owl hooted as it flew by her on silent wings, making her jump, and she turned and looked at the castle, nervously wondering if she should turn back. But if she did, she would learn nothing.

The grass beneath her feet was tufted with hillocks that made the going uneven, and once or twice she stumbled as her foot caught in a ditch. Then her shin hit against something hard and she found that she had reached a low wall. She felt along it with her hands until she found a gap and went through.

The light was now further away and she hurried forward, only to trip over a large stone. When she looked down, she dimly made out the shape of a headstone. It had fallen on to its side and lay, neglected, on the turf. She stepped back in alarm, and found the back of her legs were against another tomb. Icy fingers of fear crawled up her spine. She was in a graveyard.

She wished she was safely in her own room, in front of the fire, reading about knights and battles, but as her panic began to dissipate, she reminded herself that it was only seven o'clock, and that there was probably a down-to-earth explanation for the lantern, which she would soon discover.

The light had disappeared and she moved forward cautiously. Her footsteps halted. She could see a figure kneeling ahead, silhouetted against the lantern, which was on the ground. As she stood there uncertainly, the moon sailed out from behind a cloud, and in the cold light she saw that the figure was Lord Torkrow. To her shock, his shoulders were heaving, and she realized he was crying.

Her heart lurched at the desolate sound, and she found herself privy to a terrible grief. She was torn between a desire to leave and an impulse to go and comfort him, but caught between the two impulses she remained where she was.

She was frozen, lost in a timeless expanse, until at last his grief was spent. His cries subsided and he stood up, reclaiming his lantern. Helena shrank back against the gravestone and he passed by without seeing her, his lantern bobbing away from her in the dark.

When he had gained a sufficient lead she followed the light back across the moors, back through the arch and back to the castle. She slipped round the side to the small door and let herself in, her fingers trembling as they lifted the latch.

What had she just witnessed? she asked herself. Was it grief for the loss of a loved one, or could there a more sinister explanation? Could it be that his tears had been produced by guilt?

As she slipped upstairs, she felt the atmosphere of the castle beginning to oppress her.

She took off her outdoor clothes, glad to be safe in her room. But as she sat down by the fire, Lord Torkrow's desolate cries echoed in her ears.

5

Helena dreamt that she was outside, late at night, and flying across the moor. Above her was a gibbous moon, with torn clouds blowing across its face, and ahead of her was a blasted tree, its twigs spreading like fingers and its joints creaking as it was bent and twisted by the wind. She sped towards it, then passed through the branches and emerged untouched on the other side. Before her lay a graveyard, with tombs scattered across it like bones picked clean by the crows. Beside them was a man, wrapped in a cloak, with a lantern at his side. As she glided closer, she saw that his face was ghostly. Black shadows filled the hollows, and a sickly pallor marked the planes. He was shaking with grief, and his shoulders were heaving as racking sobs filled the air. She flew closer, around and behind him, until she was looking over his shoulder into the grave.

Then all of a sudden she realized his shoulders were shaking, not with grief, but with mirth and, as she looked past him, she saw, to her horror, that the body in the grave was that of her aunt. She turned and fled, moving rapidly away, carried on the wind, floating higher and higher as she approached the castle, rising up and up, until she was on a level with the attic, and she found herself looking through the windows. There was nothing to be seen, only the ghostly shapes of furniture cloaked in dust sheets, and a clock ticking, ticking by the wall. And then a dust sheet moved, and was thrown back, and her aunt's corpse rose from a chair.

Helena awoke with a shock. She was covered in cold sweat and was trembling all over. It was icy in the room. She shivered, and her breath formed clouds in front of her. With numb fingers she reached out for her wrapper and threw it round her shoulders, then climbed out of bed on shaking legs. She went over to the fire, which had all but gone out. She raked the ashes, encouraging a small spark, and fed it with small pieces of paper. She piled on twigs, and when they had caught light she put on a few pieces of coal. Still shivering, she returned to her bed . . . but she stopped as she approached it, for there was something under the covers. Her skin began to crawl. She saw the covers rise and fall. Someone was under there!

Someone, or some thing.

She reached out and twitched back the cover, and her aunt sat up in the bed, two weeks dead and laughing —

She sat up with a start.

Am I really awake this time? Helena wondered, her heart hammering in her chest. Or am I still dreaming? She looked around the room, fearing another nightmare vision, but everything was peaceful. The fire was burning low in the grate, casting a mellow glow over the furniture. All was as it should be. Her pulse began to slow, and her breathing became less shallow. She reached for her wrapper, still not convinced that she was awake. Warily, she threw it round her shoulders and slipped out of bed. She went over to the fire and knelt down beside it, warming her hands and taking comfort from the glowing coals. She lit a candle, then sat on the hearth, loath to go back to bed. She glanced towards it, but there was no strange shape under the covers. The blanket was still thrown back, revealing the white sheets beneath.

She heard the clock strike in the hall. It would soon be time for her to rise. She was glad of it. She had no desire to go back to bed. She waited only for Effie to bring her hot water and relight the fire before slipping out of her nightgown and, once washed, putting on her dress. Having completed her toilette, she left the room. The stone corridor was unwelcoming. Her candle seemed feeble, a puny attempt to light the space. Walls and ceiling waited in the shadows. The castle seemed a living thing. Old, monstrous, biding its time, before it claimed another victim.

She tried to banish such thoughts, but they would not leave her. She quickened her steps and the patter of her feet was matched by the patter of her heart.

Quicker and quicker, down the stairs, through the hall, into the kitchen, where sanity was restored. Candles filled the space with light. The hearty fire added its glow. Mrs Beal was brewing a pot of tea, a beacon of homeliness in the brooding atmosphere of the castle.

'It's colder this morning,' said Mrs Beal cheerily, as she put the finishing touches to the table, adding a pot of honey to the rolls and butter that were already there. 'There was frost on the inside of the window when I came downstairs. It's still there, look, even now.'

'Yes,' said Helena, relieved to be talking about something so ordinary after her disturbed night.

She blew out her candle and put it on the dresser.

'There now, we're ready,' said Mrs Beal, looking at her handiwork with pleasure.

Helena sat on one side of the table, and Mrs Beal sat opposite her.

'Tell me, Mrs Beal, do you have a key to the east wing of the attic?' Helena asked, for she knew she must unravel its secrets soon, or say goodbye to sleep. 'I would like to air it, but the door is locked and there isn't a key on my ring.'

'No, I don't have any keys for upstairs. Now if you find you're missing a key to the wine cellar or the dairy, I can help you there. I've the keys for all the rooms below stairs.'

'No, thank you, it's only the attic key I need. Do you know if Mrs Carlisle kept any spare keys anywhere?'

Effie dropped a handful of cutlery, which clattered against the flags.

Mrs Beal shook her head and tut-tutted as the girl picked up the kitchen utensils.

'Sorry, Mrs Beal,' gasped Effie.

'Just you make sure you clean everything properly,' said Mrs Beal.

'Yes, Mrs Beal.'

'Now what were we talking of?' asked Mrs Beal.

'The key to the attic. I wanted to know if Mrs Carlisle had a spare set.'

'Not that I know of. She was a very organized lady, though, and I'm surprised there's a key missing are you sure it's not on the ring?'

'Quite sure.'

'It's possible she never had one. Some of the rooms are never used. They probably haven't been opened since her ladyship was alive.'

'Her ladyship? Did his lordship have a wife?' asked Helena, thinking that here was the answer to the mystery of him crying over a grave.

'Lor' bless you, no, his lordship's never been married,' said Mrs Beal. 'I meant her old ladyship, his mother. Ah, a wonderful woman she was. A great lady. Always had a kind word for everyone. 'That was a very good stew you served us up yesterday, Mrs Beal', or 'I want to thank you for all your hard work, Mrs Beal. The banquet was a great success'.'

'So his lordship never married,' mused Helena.

'He never needed to, not with his brother — '

She stopped suddenly.

'I didn't know he had a brother,' said Helena.

'Oh, yes. But you don't want to hear about all that,' said Mrs Beal. She took the kettle from the fire and made the tea.

'On the contrary, I'm interested in the family,' said Helena, and waited for the cook to go on.

Mrs Beal looked to be weakening, but there was another clatter as Effie dropped a pan and Mrs Beal's attention was distracted.

'What are you doing?' asked Mrs Beal, going over to the young girl.

'Sorry, Mrs Beal,' gasped Effie.

'That pan's given years of good service, and if it's properly looked after it'll give years more,' said Mrs Beal admonishingly.

'Yes, Mrs Beal,' said Effie, picking up the pan and putting it back into the sink.

Mrs Beal returned to the table, grumbling about the difficulty of finding good help in such an isolated spot. Helena tried to induce her to talk about his lordship's family again, but Mrs Beal had evidently decided that discretion was called for, and Helena could not persuade her to say more.

Instead, Mrs Beal recounted the troubles of her position, talking about the likelihood of the fishmonger retiring, and the scandalous way the dairymaids paid attention to the farm hands instead of keeping their minds on churning butter.

As she talked, Helena listened with only half an ear as she wondered about Lord Torkrow's brother. He must be a younger brother, otherwise he would have inherited the title. She wondered if he was still at school: that would explain why he was not living at Stormcrow Castle.

But she still found it odd that Mrs Beal did not want to talk about him, unless he was the black sheep of the family.

Such a fantastic idea was ridiculous, she told herself, looking round the cosy warmth of the kitchen. She resolutely banished it from her mind. But once she left the kitchen's safety and comfort, her dreams returned to haunt her. In the cold stone corridors they did not seem so far-fetched. The castle was dark and mysterious. It was also very old. It must have seen some terrible things. And so must the graveyard.

She knew she would have no peace until she had visited it again. She decided to go past it on her way to the village, in order to see Mrs Willis about appointing some maids, and read the inscription on the tombstone. If it bore the inscription H Carlisle . . . she could think no further. First, she must find out who it belonged to, then she could worry.

There were some tasks that she needed to complete first, but she resolved to go after lunch.

True to her resolve, she set out as the clock

on the stables chimed one. She paused at the threshold. A light rain was falling. Lifting her hood, she made sure it covered her head, tucking in a stray wisp of hair, then she set out across the courtyard. From the direction of the stables she could hear the muffled sound of horses snorting, but there was no other sound in the stillness.

It was cold and wet underfoot, and she was glad of her stout boots. The drizzle was dispiriting. The clammy air made her face damp, and her cloak was soon beaded with water. She went under the arch and then across the moor until she reached the low wall she had struggled over the night before. She saw the gap and went through, trying to remember the direction she had taken. She had walked forward until she had tripped over a fallen headstone . . . she saw it . . . and then she had moved forward again.

She walked more slowly, hoping to find the exact spot, but the rows of graves all looked the same. She stopped when she thought she had reached the right place and examined the tombs and headstones. There was nothing remarkable about them. Some were simple and some were ornate. Some told of long lives, and some of short. John Taylor, Bella Watson and Henry Carter had all lived for more than ninety years. Richard and Lucinda

Pargeter had died before they were twenty-two. But she could see nothing that would account for Lord Torkrow's grief, nor could she see anything bearing the name Carlisle.

She walked slowly through the graveyard, looking for any signs of a recent burial, but she could not see any disturbed earth. The graves were all at least a year old, and most of them were much older.

She began to feel more easy, knowing that her aunt had not been consigned to the ground. She felt ridiculous for having pictured Lord Torkrow as a murderer who had visited the grave of his victim, over-whelmed by remorse, when instead he was simply a taciturn man, who was at that very moment probably doing nothing more alarming than taking luncheon and dealing with his business for the day. As for the grave he had been crying over, it was a private matter, and she should not meddle in it.

Leaving the graveyard behind, she continued on her way to the village. She walked briskly, enjoying the warmth her movement brought her. She had need of it, for the drizzle had intensified and she bent her head against it. She only hoped it would not rain until she reached her destination.

She was not to be so fortunate. Before long it was raining steadily. The rain came down more and more heavily, and she was just wondering whether she had better turn back when she heard an 'Urgh!' and, raising her head, she saw a woman hurrying along the road towards her. The woman was wrapped in a cloak and wore a bonnet on her head. She looked up and their eyes met. They smiled briefly, two strangers acknowledging the dreadful weather, and Helena was emboldened to ask, 'How far is it to the village?'

'It's a tidy step, and there's more rain to come,' said the woman, looking at the darkening sky. She hesitated, and then added, 'If you would like to take shelter, my cottage is not far away.' She glanced to her left, where a track ran off from the road.

Helena hesitated, but her cloak was sodden and if she remained out of doors she would soon be soaked to the skin.

'Thank you,' she said.

The two women fell into step and turned off the road. The track was rutted, and they trod carefully, trying to keep out of the mud and puddles. Before long they came to the cottage. It was a sturdy building of stone, with small windows set deeply into the thick walls. There was a wall around the garden, and a gate was set into it. The garden contained a few hardy shrubs which were looking as bedraggled as Helena felt, and she was glad when they reached the door. The woman opened it and they stepped inside.

The hall was small, but it was clean and well cared for. The woman removed her pelisse, bonnet and gloves and hung them on a peg, then turned to Helena.

'I am Mary Debbet,' she said, laughing as she pushed her wet hair out of her eyes, 'and I am very pleased to make your acquaintance.'

'I am . . . Elizabeth Reynolds,' said Helena, wishing that she did not have to lie. 'I am the new housekeeper at the castle.'

She thought Mary might withdraw, and tell her she would be welcome to sit in the kitchen until the rain stopped, but instead Mary said, 'Here, let me help you off with your wet things.'

She helped Helena remove her sodden cloak, and hung it up to dry, then led the way to a door on their left. She paused with her hand on the door knob.

'You will meet my brother in the sitting-room,' Mary went on. 'Please, do not be offended if he does not get up. He was wounded at Waterloo, and his nerves have not recovered. The doctor prescribed complete rest, and that is why we have taken a cottage on the moors.'

'I understand,' said Helena.

Mary opened the door and they went into the sitting-room. It had rough walls painted in shades of cream, and oak beams supported the ceiling. The small window was latticed, and the window ledges were very deep. To the right was a large fire, and in front of it sat a gentleman of perhaps five and thirty years.

'We have a visitor,' said Mary.

He looked up, but did not stand.

'Mrs Reynolds is the new housekeeper at the castle,' she said.

'I am pleased to meet you,' he said. His speech was slurred, but his words were polite and sounded genuine. He held out his hand, but it trembled and he dropped it again.

'Please, do sit down,' said Mary to Helena. She rang the bell, and a neat maid appeared. 'Tea, Jane, please. We are cold and wet and need something to cheer us.'

Jane bobbed a curtsey and withdrew.

'I hope your business was not urgent,' said Mary, glancing out of the window, where the rain poured down. 'I think you will be with us for some time.'

'No, luckily it can wait. It is very good of you to take me in.'

'On the moors, we help each other,' said Mary. 'We have to. It is very different from living in a town. Out here, it is possible to freeze to death when the snow falls, and whilst I don't believe it's possible to drown, it is certainly very unpleasant when the heavens open.'

The maid returned with a tray, and Mary poured the tea. She was a beautiful young woman. Her dark hair was sparkling with raindrops, which clung to it like diamonds. It was drawn back from her face in a tight chignon, but the severity of the style only served to enhance the beauty of her face. She had a creamy complexion and dark eyes. Her cheekbones were high, and her nose and mouth were well shaped. Her figure was good, and her well-cut gown suited her. She must have had many suitors in town, and Helena found it admirable that she had chosen to accompany her brother to an isolated spot for the good of his health, rather than indulge in the frivolities that must have been her lot in a more civilized location.

'Did you have some shopping to do in the village?' Mary asked.

'No,' said Helena, sipping her tea. 'I was going to see Mrs Willis, to ask her if she could help me to find some maids.'

'Ah.'

'There were girls working at the castle until recently, but they left, and I am finding it difficult to manage without them.'

'Yes, I'm sure you are. The castle is very large to manage alone. But it isn't surprising the girls left. There is a lot of superstition hereabouts. They were frightened of the strange noises in the attic, and instead of attributing them to the creaking of old wood and the sighing of the wind, they attributed them to ghosts and ghouls.'

'You know about that?' asked Helena in surprise.

'There is not much to talk about in a small village,' said Mary with a smile. 'We all know everything. Tell me, have you heard any chains rattling or children crying? They are apparently everyday sounds at the castle.'

'No,' said Helena, smiling, too, at Mary's humorous tone of voice.

'You do not seem very happy, however,' said Mary, her expression becoming more serious. 'I don't suppose the castle is really haunted?'

'No, of course not,' said Helena quickly.

'But there is something troubling you,' said Mary thoughtfully.

Helena put down her cup.

'There are noises,' Helena admitted. 'But they are just the noises typical of an old building. It is taking me some time to get used to it, however. I have never lived in a castle before.'

'It must be exciting,' said Mary.

'I believe it would be, if I did not have so much work to do' — and if I was not so worried about my aunt, she added to herself.

'Yes, it must be difficult to keep clean. Old buildings always are. I hope you find the servants you need — though they may not be much use. Mrs Carlisle had a hard time making them work, I believe. They were more interested in gossiping, or so she told me.'

'Did you know her?' asked Helena in surprise.

'Oh, yes, we both did. We were very fond of Mrs Carlisle. She was an intelligent and interesting woman. We made her acquaintance at church, and she was good enough to visit us when she had an afternoon off. We do not have much company, and her visits were a treat for us, until . . . '

'Until?'

'Until they stopped.' Mary picked up the teapot. 'Would you like another cup of tea?'

'Yes, please.'

Mary poured the tea, but did not continue.

'It must have been disappointing for you,' said Helena, prompting her.

'Yes, indeed. I asked Lord Torkrow if she was ill, thinking this must be why she had not called, and he said — '

'Yes?'

'He said she had gone to care for a sick sister and would not be returning.' Mary hesitated, and Helena had the feeling she was going to say that she did not believe in the story of the sick sister. She was clearly troubled, but did not seem to know how to begin. Then her expression changed, and Helena guessed that her sense of propriety had won out over her need to talk about her anxieties. Instead of expressing any fears, she simply said, 'It is a pity.'

'It is indeed,' said Helena.

There was a pause and then, in a slightly artificial tone of voice, Mary said, 'I am sorry not to have seen her one last time. We have a poetry book of hers, which she kindly lent to my brother.'

'I didn't know my — ' Helena stopped herself saying *aunt* just in time, 'predecessor liked poetry.'

'Oh, yes, she was a very cultured woman. Do you have a forwarding address?' she asked casually.

How clever, thought Helena, admiring Mary's subterfuge.

'No, I'm afraid I don't.'

'No matter. How are you finding it working with Lord Torkrow? I believe he is a difficult man,' she said, changing the subject.

'I have seen very little of him. As I am new,

though, everything seems strange.'

The conversation moved on, but Helena was sure that Mary's question had been a ruse. She had no doubt that Mary would have liked to write to her aunt, to reassure herself that everything was all right. So Mary, too, was anxious. Helena kept waiting for her to return to the subject, but she did not raise it again. Mary, she suspected, was in a similar position to her own: she did not know whom to trust.

They spoke of the moors, of the weather, and of Mr Debbet's health, and an hour passed very pleasantly. The rain began to abate at last.

'Thank you for your hospitality, but I think I must be going,' said Helena, as a weak gleam of sunshine found its way into the room.

'Of course,' said Mary. 'You will not walk to the village now, I hope? The light is fading, and it will soon be dark.'

'I must,' said Helena regretfully.

'Tom, our man, will be driving to the village tomorrow in the trap. I can have him take a note to Mrs Willis if you care to write one. I don't like to think of you walking on the moors so late in the day. The road is not well marked, and you might become lost on your return.'

Helena thanked her gratefully and accepted her kind offer. Mary gave her paper and pen, and Helena composed a note to Mrs Willis, asking her to send any willing girls to the castle. She particularly asked her to try and secure the return of the girls who had worked there before. She gave the note to Mary, and then the two of them went out into the hall.

'It was lucky for me I met you this afternoon,' said Helena.

'On the contrary, it was lucky for me. We see very few people. My brother, I know, enjoyed your company. He says very little but his spirits improve with diversion. I hope you will call on us again. You are welcome at any time.'

Helena thanked her, then having donned her outdoor things she took her leave. As she retraced her steps to the castle, she felt heartened to have met Mary. She felt, at least, that she had a friend in the neighbourhood, someone she could turn to if she had need. She was convinced that Mary was worried about her aunt's sudden disappearance, and decided that the next time they met she would broach the subject. If all went well, she might be able to take Mary into her confidence. Perhaps if she learnt nothing from Sally and Martha, she and Mary could think of what to do next.

She returned to the castle feeling tired, but happier than she had been for days.

Her happiness faded as she reached the courtyard however, for there, looking down at her from an upstairs window, was Miss Parkins. Seen in the distance, Miss Parkins looked like a statue, and even in the dim light, Helena felt sure the maid was watching her. She could feel the maid's malignancy spreading out to cover her.

What is she doing at the castle? thought Helena. Does she really have a hold over Lord Torkrow? Does she know something to the detriment of his brother? Is that why he allows her to remain?

Helena went on.

I might have an ally in Mary, she thought, but I have an enemy in Miss Parkins.

As she crossed the courtyard, she saw Lord Torkrow was just emerging from the front door. He was swathed in his black coat, which flapped around his ankles. She found him a conundrum. He treated her with hostility, yet he had shown her sudden gleams of friendship; he frequented graveyards at night, but once there, he was overcome with grief; he inspired fear in his neighbours, but respect in his servants.

As she looked at him, she thought to herself, Enemy or ally, which is he?

6

Helena was just about to go in the side door when she heard the sound of wheels on gravel and, turning her head, she saw that a carriage was arriving at the castle. By the check in Lord Torkrow's step, and by the fact that he was wearing his cloak, she guessed the visitors had not been expected. The carriage rolled to a halt. The coachman jumped down from the box and opened the door, and a beautifully slippered foot set itself on the step. A moment later, a young woman robed in an emerald cloak with a trim of swansdown emerged. She had flame-red hair, which was elaborately coiffured, and which was topped by a hat with a large plume. She was followed out of the carriage by an older woman, who had the same brilliant hair, and who was dressed in an equally fashionable, if more matronly style, with an amber pelisse and turban.

Helena slipped in the side door and went upstairs to remove her cloak. As she did so, she passed Miss Parkins on the landing. Miss Parkins was looking down at the party below.

'He should have married her,' said Miss Parkins suddenly.

Helena did not know if the maid was speaking to her, and so she did not reply.

'*His* parents wished it,' said Miss Parkins, with a trace of bitterness. '*Her* parents wished it. It was a good match for both of them. If he had married her, he would have been on honeymoon when . . . '

The sound of tinkling laughter came up from below, as the guests entered the hall. Miss Parkins seemed to recollect herself and she turned to Helena.

'You will have to hurry. You will be wanted downstairs.'

'Will you not be helping?' asked Helena.

Miss Parkins's gaze rested on Helena, making her squirm inwardly.

'His lordship and I do not see eye to eye on the subject of Miss Fairdean. He will not require my presence.'

'And Dawkins?'

'Dawkins has gone on an errand for his lordship.'

'Very well,' said Helena.

Miss Parkins moved away, leaving a chill behind her, making Helena shiver.

Helena returned to her room, removing her cloak and tidying her hair. As she did so, she regarded herself in the cheval glass. She had a well-shaped face with fine eyes and was passably pretty, as pretty, perhaps, as Miss

Fairdean, but there any similarity between them ended. Miss Fairdean's hair had been arranged in the most becoming coiffure, artistically arranged with small curls framing her face, whereas Helena's chignon was scraped back from her face, with no curls to soften the style. Miss Fairdean's cloak had been made of velvet, and had shimmered like an emerald in the dim light, whereas Helena's cloak was made of grey wool. Her dress, too was made of dark grey wool, and she found herself wondering what Miss Fairdean's gown would be like.

Just for a moment she longed for beautiful clothes. She had never worn silk or satin; never possessed anything made out of velvet or lace; and never had a colour more interesting than dark blue. Miss Fairdean's hair and fashionable clothes had brightened up the afternoon like a beacon, whereas her own appearance was as dreary as the weather.

Fortunately, she had no time to linger. She could do nothing about her dull appearance, and besides, she had work to do. She went downstairs. The bell was ringing in the drawing-room as she reached the hall, and she answered it promptly. She went in to see Miss Fairdean reclining elegantly on a *chaiselongue*, her well-cut morning gown showing off her Rubenesque curves. She reminded Helena of a painting she had once seen in London, voluptuous and enticing, like a Venus come down to earth. Her mother, who was still a handsome woman, sat beside her.

Helena's eyes turned to Lord Torkrow, who was standing on the other side of the fireplace. His body was blocking the firelight, and cast a black shadow across the gold damask-covered chair.

To her surprise, he was not looking at Miss Fairdean, he was looking at her. His eyes were fixed on her for fully a minute, as though committing her to memory. So long did he look, that Miss Fairdean and her mother looked, first at him, and then at Helena. They exchanged glances, and Miss Fairdean gave one exquisite shrug of her shoulder.

He roused himself.

'Mrs Reynolds,' he said. 'Some refreshments for my guests.'

'Very good, my lord.'

'You have managed to find a new housekeeper, I see,' said Miss Fairdean, as Helena walked towards the door.

'I have.'

'At least this one isn't as ugly as the last one,' said Miss Fairdean. 'The last one was a dreadful woman. She had a sour face, as though she'd been drinking vinegar. It must have been a torment for you to have to look at her. Where the offices find such frights is beyond me.'

Helena felt her teeth clench and, happening to glance in the mirror hanging by the door, she noticed that Lord Torkrow was watching her with a curious expression on his face. She quickly smoothed her expression and went out of the room, but Miss Fairdean's words would not leave her. A sour face? thought Helena angrily. Her aunt was a beautiful woman. She was lined with age and hard work, it was true, but beautiful nonetheless.

She hurried down to the kitchen.

'Tea, please, and cakes, Mrs Beal,' she said, when she entered the kitchen. 'We have visitors.'

Mrs Beal looked at her and then said, 'Miss Fairdean?'

Helena was surprised. 'How did you guess?'

'She's made you angry, and there's only one person round here that can anger a body so soon. What was she saying?'

'She made a remark about Mrs Carlisle,' said Helena bitterly.

'Ah. She's a spoilt young woman,' said Mrs Beal, as she set the kettle over the fire. 'His lordship's parents wanted him to marry her, but he was having none of it. They couldn't understand it. But fair by name is not fair by nature, and I reckon his lordship can tell the difference between the two.'

Mrs Beal set cups and saucers on the tray, followed by the tea pot, milk jug and sugar bowl. Helena carried them upstairs to the drawing-room. When she went in, a lively discussion was taking place.

'Oh, do say you'll let it go ahead,' said Miss Fairdean in an enticing voice. 'The spring won't be the same without a costume ball. It is such a feature of the castle. It is not such a very great amount of work, and besides, half of it must already be done.' She leant towards Lord Torkrow. 'Do say it will go ahead.'

Lord Torkrow turned to Helena.

'Miss Fairdean would like me to host a costume ball at the castle,' he said. 'Traditionally, we have one here each spring. I decided to cancel it this year when my housekeeper left, but perhaps it is not necessary. What do you think of the idea?'

'It is not my place to say,' said Helena, surprised that he had asked her.

'Really, how very eccentric, asking the housekeeper,' said Mrs Fairdean with a startled, and not altogether pleased, expression.

'It will be Mrs Reynolds's place to do the

work,' he said. 'Why shouldn't she have a say?'

'My dear Lord Torkrow, she is paid to do it, as she is paid to do whatever your heart desires.'

'Whatever my heart desires? If she can do that, then she is cheap at twice the price,' he said.

Miss Fairdean looked confused, unable to understand his speech, and his words darkened the air.

'It is for you to decide, my lord,' Helena said.

'Is it? I think not. Not before I know something more about you. Have you ever organized a costume ball before?' He turned to his guests. 'Mrs Reynolds comes to me with three years' experience of housekeeping, but she has never been in such a large establishment. It takes a certain kind of woman to make a success of such a venture.'

Helena did not know why he was behaving so strangely; whether he wanted to flurry her into saying something that would reveal she was not a housekeeper, or whether he wanted to discomfit his guests. His manner to them was polite, but there were hidden barbs beneath the surface, and she suspected he did not like them. Mrs Fairdean had looked uncomfortable at first, but now ignored his

113

strange manner, as did her daughter.

'No, my lord, I have not,' Helena replied.

'What does that signify?' asked Miss Fairdean impatiently. 'She can learn. Please, Simon, let us have one,' she went on in a wheedling voice. 'I have thought of my costume already.'

'I suppose it is very beautiful?' he asked her.

Helena was shocked to hear that he spoke with barely concealed contempt, but Miss Fairdean did not seem to notice.

'It is,' she said coquettishly.

'Then we must not disappoint you. Mrs Reynolds, you will continue with the arrangements for the costume ball. It will be held at the start of next month. You will engage any extra staff you need to help you. Miss Fairdean will delight us all with a beautiful costume, and I . . . '

'Yes?' said Mrs Fairdean encouragingly.

'I will come as a crow.'

Miss Fairdean looked startled, but then she carried on as though he had not said anything.

'We must move quickly, Mama. That sluggard of a seamstress must be made to work harder. She is always dragging her heels, and making some excuse or other. She is idle, like all of her kind. We will make her see she must work for her money. We will go to London tomorrow and chivvy her. There are gloves to buy, jewels to be set . . . '

Helena poured the tea whilst they continued to talk about the ball, roundly abusing the seamstresses, wig makers, milliners and shopkeepers who would provide them with everything they needed. Lord Torkrow said nothing, but the Fairdeans did not seem to notice. Helena, having poured the tea, returned to the kitchen.

'I've just learnt we're to arrange a costume ball for the start of next month,' she said

'Ah, so he's going ahead with it, is he?' asked Mrs Beal. 'I thought the Fairdeans wouldn't want him to cancel it, but I'm surprised he gave in to them so easily. He's never liked that sort of thing.'

'When are we to hold it?' asked Helena.

'On the third,' said Mrs Beal. 'And a lot of work it will be. Did Mrs Willis say she would find out some maids?'

'I didn't speak to her,' said Helena. 'It was raining too heavily and I had to turn back. But I managed to send a message to her.' She didn't mention Mary. She felt instinctively that the fewer people who knew about Mary the better. She felt safer for having a place to run to, should she need it. 'What has been arranged so far?' she asked.

'The invitations have all been written, and the guests have all very likely had their costumes made. The ball's held every year, it's a big event hereabouts, and everyone looks forward to it.'

'The food will not have been ordered?'

'No. That's something that will have to be done, and done soon. We'll need a sight of meat and vegetables, and eggs, we must have plenty of eggs — there'll be puddings to make, and custards and meringues. Cream, too,' she said. 'Ah, well, the shopkeepers are expecting it, that's one thing in our favour, they'll see to it we have everything we need. A chance for them to make some money, it is, and that's always welcome.'

'Who sees to the wine?' asked Helena.

Mrs Beal shook her head.

'Dawkins,' she said. That one word conveyed her dissatisfaction, and Helena guessed that he drank the wine he was meant to guard.

'He has the key to the wine cellar?' asked Helena.

'One of them. I keep the other one. I look in every week, to make sure that not too much has gone missing.'

'I'm surprised his lordship does not want a butler.'

'His lordship's lost heart, since . . . Ah,

well, it was a long time ago, and he never bothered to replace the butler when he left. 'Dawkins can manage', he said.'

Her tone plainly said that Dawkins could not manage, but that she could do nothing about the situation.

'Now, about the desserts . . . '

They fell to discussing the arrangements, until the bell rang again.

'They'll have finished with the tea tray,' said Mrs Beal.

Helena returned to the drawing-room, and to her surprise she found that Lord Torkrow's visitors had gone. Only the used tea cups and the hollows in the furniture showed they had ever been there.

'Mrs Reynolds. Come in.'

The fire had burnt down low, and its flames created odd patches of light across his body, throwing one shoulder and one side of his face into relief. His forehead, chin and cheek were lit brightly, and a gleam of gold was awakened in his eye. He turned his face to hers, and she wondered why she had never noticed how fine his cheeks were. They were like the rocks outside, sharp-angled, but with the stone made smooth by the constant onslaught of the elements.

'You have been speaking to Mrs Beal about the ball?' he asked.

117

'Yes, my lord.'

'Good. She has been here for many years, and knows what is required. Your predecessor had already done much of the work. You will find her notes in the housekeeper's room, no doubt. You have spoken to Mrs Willis about finding some more maids?'

'No, my lord. I was driven back by the weather. But I managed to send her a note, asking her to help me find two girls.'

'You will need more than two maids if the ball is to go ahead. You had better go and see her tomorrow, and tell her of the change of plan.'

'Yes, my lord.'

He stood there, saying nothing more, and Helena was conscious of a disturbing atmosphere in the room. It was as though he was keeping himself on a tight rein, and she felt that if he let the reins go, the power released would change her life for ever.

He considered her intently, and then he surprised her by saying, 'You were in the graveyard last night.'

Her heart jumped at the unexpected shift in the conversation. She wondered if he had seen her, or if someone else had told him.

'It's a strange place for a young woman to be after dark,' he continued. 'What were you doing there?'

'I went out for a breath of air,' she answered. 'I did not know where I was going. I walked across the courtyard and then on to the moor.'

'And just stumbled across the graveyard?'

She hesitated, wondering what to say. It would be easier to let him think she had found it by accident, but she wanted to say something, something that would help him, for she knew that he had been in pain. And he was still in pain now. She could see it etched across his face, in the lines around his mouth and by the haunted look in his eyes.

She heard herself saying, 'I was drawn to it by the sound of someone crying.' He went pale, but gave no other sign that he had been the person crying by the grave. She went on, 'I wanted to comfort them. It is a desolate thing, to cry alone, in the dark.'

His eyes locked on to hers and she felt something pass between them. Won't he tell me? she wondered, without even knowing what it was she wanted him to say, only that he had secrets, and burdens, and she felt she could help him carry them if he would only let her.

With the question, she no longer felt like a housekeeper talking to her employer, she felt like a woman talking to a man. Even so, she was unprepared for his reaction to her words.

He suddenly grasped her hand and, saying, 'Come with me', he pulled her along behind him, out of the room, up the broad, shallow stairs, so quickly that she had to run to keep up with him; along the corridor and into the portrait gallery. Then he let her go.

She looked about her. A long line of Torkrows hung on the wall. These were the men who had built the castle. They were also the men who had given rise to the tales in the village; superstitious nonsense most likely, arising from nothing more than the family living in a castle, and coming and going at will. Or so she tried to reassure herself.

The portraits began many centuries before. There were maidens in wimples and men in doublet and hose. There were cavaliers in silk and satin, and ladies in velvet and lace. There were men in tailcoats and women in panniered gowns; family portraits and wedding portraits; old men and little children. She traced the progression of family features, from the first Lord Torkrow to the man beside her.

There were several recent paintings of him. The first showed his family: his father and mother with their three children, two boys and a girl. He and his brother looked to be about the same age, whilst the girl appeared to be three or four years younger. His brother was like their mother, fair-haired and blue-eyed, and looked like a cherub, whilst he and his sister were dark-haired. His eyes looked out at her and she was shaken by the change in them. The eyes in the portrait were not haunted and secretive, as they were now, they were clear and happy.

Her gaze moved on until she stood in front of a portrait of the three children, fully grown, and dressed in the fashions of a few years previously. It was of the fair-haired son's wedding day. Helena remembered what Mrs Beal had said, that Lord Torkrow had no need to marry because of his brother. She must have meant that, as he had an heir in his brother, and as his brother looked set to carry on the family line, Lord Torkrow had no need to marry if he did not want to. Helena looked at the portrait of the bride, who stood next to his brother. She was a beautiful young woman with soft fair hair, and she seemed happy.

What had happened to the brother? she wondered. Where was he now? Not at school, that much was clear. So where was he? And where was his wife?

'Do you know what they call my family in the village?' he asked.

'Yes,' she acknowledged. 'They call you Stormcrow.'

She turned towards him and she was preternaturally aware of him. Though not handsome, his face was striking, and she found her eyes tracing the lines of his forehead, nose and mouth. It was not prone to laughter as it had been in his portrait, and she wondered if it would ever be again.

'Do you know why they call us that?' he asked.

She shook her head.

'Do you know what a stormcrow is?'

'No.'

'A stormcrow is a bird of ill omen,' he said. 'It brings bad news.' He led her over to the first portrait. It was of a thin, sinewy man in middle age, with bright amber eyes.

'This is the first earl. He brought the news of the Yorkist defeat at the Battle of Bosworth back to his father. As you can see, he was a man with a thin face and bright eyes. As he rode across the moors to break the news, a storm followed him. A crow flying before the storm alighted on his shoulder, and they rode in through the gate together. When it was known what news he brought, an old man, playing on our name of Torkrow, quipped, *Here they are, two stormcrows.*'

They moved on.

'That is the second earl,' he said.

He stood behind her. He lifted his hand as

they looked at the portrait, and for a moment, she thought he was going to rest it on her shoulder. She felt an awareness ripple through her in anticipation of his touch, but instead he gestured at the painting, and the lack of his touch left her feeling strangely empty.

'Richard brought his father the news that his mother was dead, thrown by her palfrey,' he continued. ''My son, you are a true stormcrow', his father said.'

Helena looked up at the face of Richard, who was dressed fashionably for his era, in a slashed doublet and breeches. He looked carefree.

'He had not earnt his nickname when this portrait was painted,' she said.

'No. He had no idea what was about to happen. He was still happy, then.'

He moved to the next portrait. The third Earl was standing with his hands on his hips and with his legs wide apart, looking solid and secure. He was wearing a doublet that accentuated the width of his shoulders, with wide sleeves that billowed outwards, before being confined at his wrist.

'He looks as though nothing can topple him, doesn't he?' asked Lord Torkrow, standing behind her. He was so close that she could feel his body heat, and she had a

123

disturbing urge to lean backwards and feel his warmth envelop her, but she resisted the strange impulse.

'What happened to him?' asked Helena.

'There was a fire, and the family house in York was razed to the ground. He brought the news to his mother, an old woman of ninety-nine, who had been making plans to celebrate her one hundredth birthday. The news caused his mother's death, three hours before she would have achieved her ambition. He was ostracized for giving his mother the news, instead of letting her hear it through other means, after her birthday.'

He went on, telling her the story of each Stormcrow, and of how each one had earned his name, until at last they stood before his own family portrait.

'And you?' asked Helena. 'How did you earn the name?'

He said nothing, and a profound silence engulfed them. Helena turned to look at him, and she saw that his face had gone white. His eyes, in contrast, were dark and hollow, and the rings around them were black. He was staring at the portrait, and she knew he was far away, back in the past. His hands had dropped to his side, and she saw that they were clenched into fists. He opened his mouth, and she thought he was going to speak, but then he turned and strode out of the gallery, leaving her alone.

She looked again at the portrait of the boy he had been, a happy, carefree child. But now he was a man sunk in mystery, and darkness wrapped itself around him like a shroud.

★　★　★

Why did I do that? Simon asked himself as he descended the massive staircase and went into the library, wondering why he had tried to make her understand.

He tried to settle to estate business, but he could not concentrate. He heard Helena's light step as she descended the stairs and went into the housekeeper's room. He picked up his quill, then threw it down and went out of the library, climbing the stairs two at a time, returning to the gallery and pacing to the end, then pressing the embossing on the wall and waiting impatiently for the secret door to open. It swung inwards ponderously, and he went inside.

The room was small and panelled. A window looked out on to the moor. An empty grate held blackened ashes. Above the fireplace hung a portrait. It was of a young woman, his brother's bride. She was looking radiantly beautiful. She wore her fair hair loose, hanging round her shoulders in soft curls. Her muslin gown, with its high waist, revealed a slight figure with gentle curves. Her lips were pink, and her eyes were blue. She was standing in a garden, and the dew was on the roses.

He stood, lost in thought, until a sound disturbed him. Miss Parkins had entered the hidden room. She was the last person he wanted to see, especially here, now.

'Did you wish to speak to me?' he asked her coldly.

'I understand you are to go ahead with the ball, my lord.'

'Yes, I am.'

'Do you think it wise? A masked ball can hide many secrets.'

'I have made my decision. The ball will go ahead.'

'Very good, my lord,' she said, with a trace of insolence.

She walked over to him and stood beside him, looking at the portrait.

'She was very beautiful,' said Miss Parkins.

'Yes, she was.' He could not keep the wistfulness out of his voice.

'Your brother chose well. He loved her dearly. Until you killed her.'

7

The following morning, Helena began to organize the castle in earnest. Unsettled by everything that had happened, she was glad to take refuge in physical labour. The library, drawing-room and dining-room were well cared for, so she decided to rescue a further room from its state of neglect. If there was to be a ball, then the castle must be brought back to life again. All thoughts of leaving quickly had left her, for she did not intend to go before she had had a chance to speak to Sally and Martha.

She chose a small sitting-room that overlooked the front of the castle, and she began by removing the dust sheets, taking them off and folding them carefully so as not to disturb the dust that had settled on them. She was surprised to see that the furniture was of good quality, and delicate. Gold chairs in elegant styles were upholstered with red brocade, a padded sofa was covered in a matching brocade, and, as she removed the dust sheets from the floor, she discovered a flowered carpet. It had been a lady's room, then, she thought, as she looked about her.

She rang the bell, and whilst she waited for it to be answered, she began to dust the mantelpiece and other surfaces, revealing the beauty of the wood beneath.

The door opened and Effie entered hesitantly.

'It's all right, Effie, come in. I am preparing this room for use. I want you to light a fire here, and then I would like you to bring a bucket of water and wash the windows. Make sure Mrs Beal does not need you first.'

'Yes, mum.'

Effie departed, but returned soon afterwards.

As they worked, Helena asked the girl about her family. Reluctantly at first, Effie began to speak, saying that she had been orphaned and that a cousin had found her work at the castle. Once or twice, Helena led the conversation round to Mrs Carlisle, but Effie became nervous when she did so, and she talked of other things. Gradually, though, she began to win the girl's trust, and thought that, before many more days had passed, she might induce Effie to confide in her. That the girl knew something she was convinced, though whether it was important remained to be seen.

By late afternoon, the room was looking cheerful. Helena had wound the ormolu clock, which was ticking on the mantelpiece, and polished the gilded mirrors. Effie had washed the windows, both inside and out, and they sparkled where they caught the light. The fire was crackling merrily in the grate.

'It's a pity there is no one to use it,' said Helena to Effie, pushing a stray strand of hair out of her eyes with the back of her hand.

'Yes, mum.'

'Whose room was it? Do you know?'

'It was 'ers,' said Effie, not very helpfully.

'Was it used by Lord Torkrow's mother?'

Effie did not reply.

'Or his sister-in-law?'

Effie nodded.

'She liked it 'ere.'

'Does she live here now?' asked Helena.

Effie dropped the poker with a clatter, and was clearly frightened.

'Where is she, Effie?' asked Helena. 'Is she in the castle? Or on holiday?'

'No, mum. She's dead.'

'Dead?'

'Yes, mum.'

'Then the crying in the attic — ' *is not her*, Helena was about to say, when Effie interrupted her.

'Yes, mum, it's 'er. Dawkins says she walks,' said Effie.

'Nonsense,' said Helena reassuringly. 'The dead don't walk, Effie. There was nothing in the attic but a cat. Together we have made a very good job of this,' she went on more cheerfully. 'The room looks bright and welcoming.'

'P'raps she'll stop crying now, mum. P'raps she'll walk in 'ere, not in the attic.'

As the thought clearly cheered her, Helena did not gainsay it.

'Now, you must return to the kitchen. I'm sure Mrs Beal will be wanting you. I will finish here.'

Effie picked up her bucket and left the room.

As Helena put a few finishing touches to the room, she wondered what had happened to Lord Torkrow's sister-in-law, thinking: How did she die? How long ago was it?

And where is she buried?

★   ★   ★

Helena joined Mrs Beal for dinner that evening, and as Mrs Beal dished out the mutton stew, she said, 'I will be going to see Mrs Willis tomorrow afternoon about finding some more maids for the castle. How many do you think I will need?'

'Take as many as you can find,' said Mrs

130

Beal. 'There's plenty of work to be done.'

'I have made a start on the downstairs rooms already, opening up a sitting-room overlooking the front of the castle. Effie tells me it used to belong to his lordship's sister-in-law. I saw her portrait in the gallery. She was very beautiful.'

'Yes, she was, poor lady.'

'It was a tragedy when she died.'

'Master Richard went mad with grief,' said Mrs Beal with a sigh, then, recollecting herself, added, 'Least said, soonest mended, I always say. You're going to see Mrs Willis this afternoon?'

'Yes.'

'You'd better ask her to help you find some footmen, too. There's going to be a lot of work fetching and carrying beforehand, and we'll need someone to carry the drinks on the day.'

'It's all rather daunting,' said Helena. 'Did Mrs Carlisle find it so?'

'Bless you no, she'd arranged a dozen balls for his lordship.'

'If only I had her sister's address, I could write to her and ask her for her advice.'

'You wouldn't want to bother her, not with her sister being so ill,' said Mrs Beal, 'and besides, you've no need to worry. It will all come right in the end.'

As Helena set out for the village after luncheon she was glad to leave the castle behind. She felt herself being drawn deeper and deeper into its tangled world, but Lord Torkrow and his family had nothing to do with her. She had come to the castle for one reason and one reason only: she wanted to find her aunt.

The day was fine, with a weak sun shining out of a blue sky, and she was pleased to see that there was no threat of rain. It was miles to the village, across the moors, so she set off at a brisk pace. Hardy sheep were grazing, and she was glad of their bleating, which broke the silence and made the walk less lonely.

As she approached the turning to Mary's cottage, she decided to take it and pay Mary a call. She longed for someone to confide in, someone outside the castle, who was immune to its strange atmosphere and past. Perhaps Mary could shed some insight on to her aunt's disappearance.

The rough track was dry, unlike the last time she had visited, when the rain had turned it to mud, and was much easier to walk on. She soon found herself outside the cottage, and knocked on the door. It was opened by the maid, but Helena quickly learnt that neither Mary nor her brother were at home, and that the maid did not know when they would be back.

Helena swallowed her disappointment, thanked the maid, asked for Mr and Miss Debbet to be told that she had called, and carried on to the village. As she approached, she passed a small cottage, and then a few more, scattered haphazardly across the harsh landscape. She passed an old woman, dressed in black, as she entered the village, and a serious-looking little boy who was carrying a large basket into a cottage.

Helena greeted them with a 'Good afternoon', but they did not reply, instead favouring her with suspicious looks.

The village was larger than she had expected, and better favoured. It was sheltered from the prevailing wind by being built in a hollow of the moors, and it consisted of a collection of cottages and houses, with an inn at one end and a church at the other. Next to the church was a large, square stone building which Helena took to be the rectory. It was set back from the road, and separated from it by a low stone wall. There was a white-painted gate which creaked as Helena opened it, and a stone path snaked between barren borders to the door.

Helena lifted the brass knocker, which fell with a satisfying clunk, and a minute later the door was opened by an elderly maid.

'I am Mrs Reynolds, the new housekeeper at the castle,' said Helena. 'I'd like to see Mrs Willis.'

The maid bade her enter, then left her in the hall. It was well cared for, and Helena took pleasure in seeing a house she did not have the responsibility of cleaning. The living was perhaps not wealthy, but it seemed to keep the rector and his wife in some comfort. The hall was painted a muted green, and there was a rug on the polished floorboards, whilst a staircase led upwards on the left.

The maid returned to say, 'Mrs Willis says, 'Please come in.''

'Thank you,' said Helena, as the maid helped her off with her cloak.

She went into the drawing-room. Whilst the hall had been plain, here there were pretensions of gentility. There was gold wallpaper on the walls, a brocade sofa, and an inlaid console table beneath the window. On it was a vase of fine porcelain, matched by two others of similar design on the mantelpiece. The candlesticks were of silver, and there was a good painting hanging above it. A square piano was set against the far wall, and a brocade-covered stool was set in front of it. A fire was burning in the grate, and the fire irons gleamed in the light of the flames.

Mrs Willis stood up. Her dress was simple yet well cut, and to Helena's surprise, it was made of silk.

'Mrs Reynolds, how very nice to meet you,' she said in a cultured voice. 'My husband and I heard there was to be a new housekeeper at the castle. It is not before time. I dread to think how his lordship has managed without one. Won't you sit down?'

Helena thanked her and took a seat.

'I have come to ask for your help,' said Helena. 'I will need some maids to assist me in the castle and, as you know the neighbourhood and the people I thought you might be able to help me find some suitable girls.'

'Ah, yes, I received your note.'

'When I wrote it, I needed only two girls, but as I now need more help, footmen as well as maids, I thought it better to come and see you in person. I understand that the two girls who worked at the castle under Mrs Carlisle left in a hurry. It is a great pity. It would have been much easier for me if they had remained,' she said.

Mrs Willis's face expressed her exasperation.

'The people round here are very insular,' she said. 'They have their prejudices and their superstitions. They mutter and whisper about Lord Torkrow, poor man, as they would mutter and whisper about anyone who lived in a castle. And the stories they tell about the castle itself! You would think it was unsafe to spend half an hour within its walls, the way some of them talk!'

Helena was reassured by Mrs Willis's disgusted manner: she, at least, did not appear to think ill of Lord Torkrow.

'I suppose it is understandable,' said Helena. 'The girls heard crying in the attic. The footman believed it to be a cat, but the girls were convinced that something dreadful had happened.'

'Exactly! That is just the sort of story I'm talking about. As if anything dreadful *would* happen.'

'It was sparked by the housekeeper's disappearance, I believe,' said Helena. 'I suppose an incident like that was bound to cause gossip. A servant does not usually leave without giving notice.'

'There was nothing suspicious about it. The poor woman left for a very ordinary reason, to tend her sick sister.'

'Did she not leave in the middle of the night? Or is that just another tale?'

'No, that is true, and of course, that fuelled the talk, but again there was a sensible reason

136

for it. There is a stagecoach to London early in the morning. I imagine she wanted to make an early start.'

'Ah, I didn't know her sister lived in London,' said Helena.

'I don't know that she does' said Mrs Willis. 'That is the stagecoach's ultimate destination, but it stops a number of times on the way. Of course, Mrs Carlisle could also have gone north, in which case she would have caught the stagecoach to Edinburgh, which passes a little later.'

'Have you heard from her?' asked Helena, with more hope than confidence.

'No. I did not know her very well. We saw each other at church; a very sensible woman, well spoken and an asset to the congregation. I helped her to find staff for the castle, but other than that I did not speak to her. I am only sorry I did not find her some girls with more common sense.'

'Do you think they would return to the castle now that I am there?' asked Helena. 'It would be a great help to have girls who know their way about.'

'Perhaps. There is little work round here. I will try and persuade them to come and see you, and if not then I will try to find you some other girls. You said that you needed more than two?'

'Yes. His lordship means to go ahead with the costume ball, so I will need as much help as possible.'

'It is to go ahead? Oh, I'm so pleased,' she said, with a spark of excitement in her eye. 'My husband and I have already chosen our costumes. We are to go as King Henry VIII and Katharine of Aragon. I have the costumes left over from another ball,' she explained. 'My husband has put on weight since then, and I have spent the last few weeks letting his costume out. I am so glad my work will not go to waste.'

'Are the balls generally large? I haven't had time to look at the guest list yet,' said Helena.

'Oh, yes, everyone from the surrounding neighbourhood is invited. They all look forward to the ball. It is a big event, in fact it is the biggest event we have in this village. The castle is something to be seen when it is *en fête*. The light pours out of the windows, and then there is the music! The orchestra is always excellent. And the food! You don't need me to tell you that Mrs Beal is an excellent cook, and on these occasions she always surpasses herself. Carriages roll up in front of the castle by the dozen, and everyone wears the most wonderful costumes. There is a great deal of imagination brought into play, and although there are always a few duplications, the local gentry for the most part try and find a more unusual character to portray.'

'Miss Fairdean and her mother have already ordered their costumes. They were at the castle yesterday,' Helena explained.

'Yes, the Fairdeans always make a special effort where the castle is concerned. They will be having their costumes made in London, I expect, complete with wigs and jewels. They will be portraying royalty, I've no doubt. Last year, Miss Fairdean dressed as Elizabeth I. With her red hair, she looked the part. Her mother must have spent a fortune on her dress. It was encrusted with pearls. I suppose she thought it was worth it. There was some talk that his lordship would marry Miss Fairdean — I believe his mother, as well as hers, wished it — but nothing has come of it. Miss Fairdean is not well liked in the neighbourhood,' she went on. 'She is very rude to her servants, and indeed to most of her neighbours. She seems to think she is above them. She said to me — ' She stopped herself, as if remembering to whom she was speaking. 'There was no call for it.'

Helena waited, hoping she would say more, but Mrs Willis was silent. Then, with the appearance of a woman turning her thoughts into new channels by an act of will, she continued.

'We will be seeing you at church, I hope? His lordship never comes, but Mrs Carlisle used to attend regularly, as long as the weather was fine enough for her to walk. She was a great supporter of the church. It was a pity she was all alone in the world, with no one to miss her when she was gone.'

Helena felt a shock at the unexpected words. *No one to miss her.*

'She had a niece, I believe?' she said quickly. 'Mrs Beal said Mrs Carlisle wrote to her niece regularly.'

'I didn't know that,' said Mrs Willis slowly.

'And then, of course, she had a sister,' said Helena.

'Oh, yes, her sister,' said Mrs Willis dismissively.

Helena was disquieted. There was something decidedly odd about Mrs Willis's manner.

The conversation moved on, but as Mrs Willis spoke about other parishioners, Helena watched her covertly. Strange stories came back to her, stories of people who disappeared mysteriously in remote places, innocent-seeming locals who were not what they appeared . . .

The chiming of the clock broke her

thoughts, and she returned to her senses. Mrs Willis was now talking about the village girls in the most matter-of-fact way, and the idea of her being mixed up in a strange disappearance seemed ridiculous.

A few minutes later, the rector, Mr Willis, entered the room. He was a stout, kindly-looking man with white whiskers, and the idea of him being mixed up in anything untoward seemed even more ridiculous than his wife's involvement.

'This is Mrs Reynolds,' said Mrs Willis, performing the introductions. After a few minutes of polite conversation, she said, 'I will do what I can for you in the village, and I will send any willing workers to see you at the castle.'

Helena thanked her, then, having taken her leave of them, she reclaimed her outdoor clothes and set out.

The day had turned colder, but it was dry, and within the hour Helena found herself once more approaching the castle. She was pleased that she had made arrangements to acquire more staff, but disappointed that she had learnt nothing of use about her aunt.

She had almost reached the outer wall when a gleam of sunshine breaking through the clouds made her look up and she let out a startled cry as she saw there was someone on the battlements. From such a distance she could not be sure if it was a man or a woman, but she meant to find out. She hurried inside and went swiftly up to the attic, thinking that she did not remember a staircase to the battlements. When she had searched the attic in the west wing she realized there wasn't one.

She wondered if someone had gone through from the east wing, or . . . She looked up, then went through the attic again, looking at the ceiling, and there, sure enough, in the corner of one room, was a small door. Tied to a handle in the middle of it was a piece of rope, and beneath it was a chair. She was about to stand on it and go through when she thought better of it, for she had no idea who was on the battlements or what they were doing there. She was just wondering what to do when she heard footsteps above her and hid herself behind a screen. Through the gap around the hinges she could still see the room. A minute later there came a creaking sound as the small door opened and a leg appeared, waving round as it tried to find the chair. Another followed, and then a pair of breeches, and then . . . Dawkins. He closed the door above him, then climbed down from the chair and put it against the wall before leaving the attic room. He was swaying as he walked, and Helena guessed what he had been doing, but she wanted to make sure. Waiting for his footsteps to die away, she replaced the chair, opened the door, and with some difficulty she climbed through.

She found herself on the battlements, with the wind whipping at her cloak and trying to pull her hair from its pins. Beneath her was the moor, grey and green in the dull light. Far off, she could see the village, with its collection of cottages and the church. She looked all round, wondering if there was any other human habitation nearby, but there was nothing except a few isolated cottages, Mary's amongst them.

Turning her attention back to the battlements, she searched them, and soon found a large cache of bottles, cushioned by sodden blankets and resting in the lee of the wall. There were perhaps a hundred bottles of wine and port, and half of them were empty. He must have taken them when the butler left, and before Mrs Beal started checking the cellars. No wonder he tried to warn people away from the attics: he did not want anyone noticing his comings and goings, or deciding to take a turn on the battlements and discovering his secret store. And if anyone heard his footsteps, why, he could blame them on a ghost.

Had it also been Dawkins crying in the attic? she wondered. She would have to try and find out.

She took one last look at the view, which was splendid from such a high vantage point, and would be even better in summer under a blue sky, and then climbed back into the attic. She grasped the piece of rope and pulled the door shut behind her, then replaced the chair and went down to her room. Once there, she took off her cloak and stout shoes, peeling off her gloves before removing her bonnet.

She was going down to the housekeeper's room when, passing the gallery, she had an urge to look at the portrait of Lord Torkrow's sister-in-law again. She went in, and had almost reached the end of the gallery when she noticed something odd. There was an open door at the end where no door should be. Curious, she went forward, and then stopped suddenly, as she saw that Lord Torkrow was in a hidden room, looking at a portrait of a beautiful girl: his sister-in-law.

Helena shrank back, then hurried from the gallery. There had been something in his face when he looked at his sister-in-law's portrait that had cut her to the heart.

She was about to go into the housekeeper's room when she changed her mind. She was tired after her exertions, and she went down to the kitchen. Mrs Beal was there, busy baking cakes.

'Well, so you're back, and cold, I'll warrant,' said Mrs Beal. 'Effie, set the kettle over the fire. How did you get on with Mrs Willis?' she asked.

'Very well. She has promised to try and find me some help, and will send any likely workers to the castle.'

'That's one job done, then,' said Mrs Beal.

The tea was made, and Mrs Beal poured it.

'I think I'll join you,' she said. 'I've some biscuits just come out of the oven. You'll have one with your tea?'

Helena thanked her, and was glad of something to eat and drink.

They fell to talking about the arrangements for the ball. Some of the suppliers had expressed doubts about being able to produce such large quantities of food, and Mrs Beal talked of alternatives whilst Helena gave her opinion.

'And now, I had better tend to my own work,' she said, as she finished her tea. 'Then, after dinner, I need to sort through the linen and make sure there are enough sheets for those guests who are staying overnight. I am hoping they are clean and dry.'

'Mrs Carlisle always took care of that.

Clean, dry and smelling of lavender, they'll be.'

Helena felt a pang as she thought of Aunt Hester, and she found she could almost smell the lavender.

'Then I had better count them and make sure we have enough.'

★   ★   ★

Helena had just reassured herself that there would be enough clean linen for the overnight guests at the ball, and was about to retire for the night, when she was startled to find Effie waiting for her in the corridor.

'Yes, Effie, what is it?'

'Please, mum, it's about the key to the attic,' said Effie, twisting her apron in her big, clumsy hands.

'Yes, Effie?'

'I knows where I thinks it is, mum.'

Helena's pulse quickened.

'Mrs Carlisle, she kept some spare keys in the scullery, missus. I saw 'er with them once. She used to go in and out of the attic, quiet-like.'

'Quiet-like, you say?' asked Helena, wondering if her aunt could have suspected Dawkins of taking wine from the cellar, and if she had perhaps followed him.

146

'Yes, missus. I saw her when I was doing the fires.'

'But you don't do the fires in the attic.'

'I was doing them in the bedrooms, mum, and I 'eard a noise. Manners — he was one of the footmen, missus, we used to 'ave ever so many footmen — he said to me, 'It's a ghost', and he dared me to go 'ave a look.'

'And do you mean to say you did it?' asked Helena, looking at Effie with surprise.

'No, mum. But later, when I saw Mrs Carlisle going up there, I thought, I'll go after 'er and see if there's a ghost, and if there is, she won't let it 'urt me, and if there isn't, I don't need to be frightened of what Manners says to me no more.'

'And did she go into the east wing?' asked Helena. 'Did she go into the locked attic?'

'Yes, missus. That's where the noises were coming from.'

'And was it a ghost?' asked Helena, hardly daring to breathe.

'Don't know, missus. There were something in there, I 'eard it, but I don't know what it was. Mrs Carlisle, she went in, and then about ten minutes later she come out again.'

'Was there anyone with her? Dawkins, perhaps?'

'No, mum, she were by 'erself.'

'Did she seem agitated?' asked Helena.

'Don't know, mum.'

'Did she seem happy?'

'Don't know, mum.'

'Did you see her face?' asked Helena.

'No. I runned down the stairs so she wouldn't see me.'

'Very well, thank you, Effie.' She added casually, 'Is Mrs Beal in the kitchen?'

'No, mum, she's gone to bed.'

'No matter, I will speak to her tomorrow. I have a few spare minutes, I think I will come down and look for the key now,' said Helena.

'Yes, mum.'

As she went down to the scullery, Helena's thoughts were racing. So her aunt had been into the east wing, and she had discovered something there. Was it Dawkins? But he had climbed out on to the battlements from the west wing. What else could it have been?

Could it have been Lord Torkrow's brother? There was something about his brother, she was sure, something no one was telling her. She thought of Mrs Beal saying he had been driven mad with grief. What if he had literally been driven mad, and his family had confined him in the attic?

She thought of Miss Parkins. What if Miss Parkins was looking after his lordship's brother? Or perhaps her aunt had been the one who was looking after him. Perhaps his mad brother killed her. Or perhaps her aunt threatened to tell someone about him, because he had killed or injured someone else.

She had time for no more thoughts. Going into the scullery, she asked Effie to show her where the key was kept. She was determined to solve the mystery of the attic once and for all. Effie took her to a drawer at the back of the scullery. Helena opened it . . . and it was empty.

Helena stood staring at the empty drawer with disbelief.

'It were there, mum. I saw it,' said Effie.

'Yes, I'm sure you did, Effie,' said Helena soothingly.

But the key had nonetheless gone. Who had taken it? thought Helena. And why?

8

The following morning brought a letter to the castle from Caroline. It came as a welcome relief to Helena to know that she was not entirely cut off from the outside world. The atmosphere in the castle was oppressive, but Caroline's letter brought the noise and bustle of Manchester back to her. She could see Caroline, in her mind's eye, sitting at the cramped table beneath the window, with its view of the noisy street and its glimpse of the canal. She could see Caroline lifting her head, as she always did, and then resting it on her hand as she watched the bakers walking past with trays on their heads and ragged children playing, and dogs scavenging for food. There would be a restlessness about her, for Caroline was always restless inside. And when Caroline had finished the letter she would have thrown her cloak over her shoulders in a swirling movement, picked up her basket and gone out, threading her way purposefully between the street merchants and other shoppers, stopping to talk to neighbours, and sending the letter, before looking longingly in the windows of the milliners on her way home.

Helena examined the seal and was relieved to see that it had not been tampered with, so it seemed that the mail went from and came to the castle undisturbed. If Aunt Hester had written to her, then it seemed unlikely the letter had been interfered with.

She broke the seal and began to read.

My dear friend.

Good. So Caroline had guessed something was wrong, and was writing in a guarded style.

I was very pleased to get your letter. What a pity you have heard nothing of H. I have had no news, either. I hope all is well and that we will soon hear something.

I have some news of my own. I secured the position with Mrs Ling and I am writing to you from her home in Chester. She is not too demanding and she treats me with respect, which is the most I can hope for.

You, however, deserve more.

I have seen our friend G several times and I hope you will see him before long, too. I have not given him your direction, but if you wish to write to him, I'm sure a letter would be most welcome.

I will await your next letter with interest.

She included Mrs Ling's address, and signed the letter Caroline.

As Helena folded it and put it in her pocket, she found her thoughts returning to Mr Gradwell. Life with him would be safe. He would help her when needed, indeed, he would help her now if he knew of her troubles, though there was little help he could give. Yet she had no desire to hurry home and confide in him. Quite the reverse, she was glad of some time away from him, for it enabled her to think more clearly.

She tried to imagine what life would be like with him. She would be the mistress of her own home, with a maid and a cook to serve her. She would have new clothes to wear, and a carriage to ride in, and she would be able to spend her time visiting and shopping and inviting friends to supper, instead of working all day long. She would have the companionship of Mr Gradwell, and there would be trips to the theatre and to the museums, and in the summer there would be picnics and outings to the seaside, but although it seemed very inviting, her heart sank at the thought of it. Perhaps she was just tired. She would not think about it for the moment. There would be time enough to think about it when she had found her aunt.

She began to draw up a plan for cleaning the castle, in the hope that Mrs Willis would find her some willing helpers, and was rewarded for her hope by the arrival at the castle of seven girls and six men, shortly before ten o'clock. On asking them their names, she was pleased to learn that Sally and Martha, the two girls who had worked at the castle before, were among them.

She went down to the kitchen to speak to them.

'There is plenty of work to be done,' she told them. 'Can you start today?'

They had all come prepared to stay, and Helena set them to work. Whilst two of the young men began polishing the silver under the direction of Dawkins, the other four took down one of the more recent tapestries and carried it outside and Helena set three of the girls to work beating it with brooms. The men then moved on to fetching buckets of water so that the rest of the girls could wash the floor. Helena dropped some sprigs of dried lavender into the water, to perfume it, then set the girls to work.

Fortunately the day was fine, and she joined the girls who were working outside. It was pleasant to be out of doors, and though the air was cold, beating the tapestry was heavy work and it soon warmed them.

'I think you have you worked at the castle before?' she asked Sally and Martha.

'That's right, missus.'

They were perhaps seventeen or eighteen years of age, and although they seemed ready enough to work, the glances they kept throwing at the younger footmen whenever they walked by suggested they would not be reliable if left alone.

'What were your duties?'

'We kept the rooms clean, missus. We dusted 'em and polished the grates and kept the fire-irons shiny. We swept the floors and made the beds.'

'Then I would like you to do the same now you have returned. Did you air the rooms before?'

'Yes, missus, some of 'em. The ones that 'ad someone in 'em.'

'Good, then you can continue to do so. Did you air the attics?'

'No, missus, we daren't go near the attics.'

'Why not?' asked Helena.

'There was noises,' said Sally.

'At night,' said Martha, with wide eyes.

'Made my blood curdle, they did,' said Sally. 'All that screeching and wailing.'

'You said it was crying,' put in one of the other girls, as she hit the tapestry with a broom.

'Screeching,' said Sally emphatically, 'and wailing.'

The story grew in the telling, and Helena was not surprised when the girl asserted that she had heard chains clanking behind the door. However, Helena believed there had been something in the girl's story.

'When did you hear it?' she asked.

'It were just before Mrs Carlisle disappeared. A week before, mebbe.'

'And you stayed in the castle a whole week with such noises?' asked Helena.

'They weren't so bad after that. Just sobbing now and then.'

'Ghost must've got a sore throat,' said one of the footmen cheekily, as he walked past on his way to the well.

'I'd like to see you spend a night there, for all your talk,' retorted the girl.

Helena was not sure what the girl had heard, and she knew she couldn't rely on what she said, but nevertheless she was sure Sally had heard something.

'Perhaps it was a cat,' suggested Helena.

'That's what Dawkins said, but it weren't no cat,' said Sally definitely.

'Was he with you when you heard it?'

'Right next to me, 'e was.'

So, the sound had not been made by Dawkins, at any rate.

In an attempt to find out more about Lord Torkrow's family, Helena tried to induce the maids to talk of them, but they answered her questions briefly and would not be drawn. Whether it was deliberate, or whether they were simply more interested in their own affairs, Helena did not know.

It was a pity, because something was tugging at her memory, and she thought it might be important, if only she could remember what it was.

At last she returned to the housekeeper's room to finish her plans. There was a lot of hard work to be done before the castle was ready for the ball.

The fire burned low, and Effie arrived with a bucket of coal to mend it.

Helena was about to ask her again what she had seen in the housekeeper's desk, when she had a better idea. Going over to the window, she toyed with the curtains, then said: 'Bring me some string from the drawer, would you please, Effie?'

Effie hesitated.

'The top drawer,' Helena prompted her.

The girl reluctantly went over to the desk, wiping her hands on her apron. She opened the drawer, and stood looking at something inside. She appeared to wrestle with herself, then blurted out incoherently: 'If someone knew something and someone 'ad said something but someone thought it wasn't what they said it was, what should they to do?'

'They should tell the housekeeper,' said Helena promptly.

'Very particular about 'er quills she was,' said Effie, looking at Helena nervously. 'Always used 'er own quills for letters.'

Yes, thought Helena, she did. She wished the girl would hurry up and tell her something she did not know.

'Always used 'er own quills, mum, but it's still 'ere.'

Helena's eyes widened as she realized what Effie was telling her. If Aunt Hester had left the castle, she would have taken her quill with her.

Lord Torkrow's ominous words came back to her: *The castle has a way of keeping people.*

Effie was looking at her with a frightened expression, and Helena quickly reassured her.

'Don't worry, Effie, Mrs Carlisle knew her sister's pens were well mended, I am sure.'

'Really, mum?'

'Yes, really.'

Effie's face shone with relief.

'I've been that worried, mum. It wasn't like 'er to go without saying goodbye. Always good to me were Mrs Carlisle.'

'I am sure she wanted to say goodbye, but did not want to wake you,' said Helena.

'Yes, mum,' said Effie, nodding.

'And now you had better go back to the kitchen. Mrs Beal will be wondering where you are.'

As soon as she had gone, Helena went out into the hall. Lord Torkrow had left the castle on horseback after luncheon, and Miss Parkins was also out of the castle, it being her day off. Their absence gave Helena an idea.

'Leave that,' she said to the footmen, who had rehung the tapestry and were preparing to take down the next one. 'I have something else for you to do.'

She took them upstairs, and then into the attic.

'The key to the attic has been lost,' she said. 'I would like you to break the door down.'

The footmen looked at each other uneasily.

'You're not afraid of ghosts, I hope?' she said with a smile.

'No, missus. But smashing a door . . . what will his lordship say?'

'His lordship has given me responsibility for the castle,' she said.

The footmen looked at each other, then shrugged and set their shoulders to the door.

After much heaving they managed to break the lock. They stood back, and Helena went in, her heart racing. She expected to find a madman, or her aunt, or a body . . . but she found nothing. The attic was empty. She went through into the room leading off from it. Again there was nothing. The entire east wing was empty, save for an assortment of discarded furniture and a few odds and ends. She did not know whether to be relieved or disappointed.

She went through the attic rooms again, looking for any signs that someone had been there recently. There was less dust in the central room, and a few items of bedding that could have been used, but it told her nothing. Whatever secrets the castle was nursing, they were no longer to be found in the east wing.

'Thank you,' she said to the footmen. 'You may return to your work downstairs.'

They departed, leaving her to wander through the rooms again. There must be something, some sign, she thought . . . But she could find nothing.

As she looked round the bare room, it seemed ridiculous to remember that she had fancied it housing Lord Torkrow's mad brother. She was ashamed of herself for such a thought. He was probably away, abroad, perhaps, or attending to business in London.

Or . . . something Mrs Beal had said came back to her. It had been nagging at her mind for some time, and now she remembered what it was.

She went down to the kitchen, asking Mrs Beal if she needed any of the maids to help her, before suggesting they take tea together.

Mrs Beal was agreeable, and they talked over the likelihood of the maids and footmen remaining at the castle.

When they had done, Helena asked casually: 'What is his lordship's name? His family name?'

'Pargeter,' said Mrs Beal. 'His lordship is Simon Pargeter. Why do you ask?'

'I was just curious,' said Helena.

But hers had been no idle curiosity. As soon as she had finished her tea, she put on her cloak and, slipping out of the side door, made her way to the graveyard. An icy wind was blowing across the moor, and she wrapped her cloak tightly round her. She crested the rise and then went through the gap in the low stone wall, where she found the grave she had been looking for. It was very simple and said, Richard Pargeter. *Master Richard*, Mrs Beal had called him. Lord Torkrow's brother. He wasn't in the attic, he was here in the graveyard. And next to him was his wife.

She heard a slight movement, and turning her head she saw Lord Torkrow sitting on his horse at the edge of the graveyard, watching her. So absorbed had she been that she had not heard his approach. Their eyes met; then he dismounted, tethered his horse to the dry stone wall and entered the graveyard.

'So. You discovered whose graves these are.'

'Yes. I'm sorry.'

He did not answer her immediately, and she did not break the silence, for he was lost in his own thoughts.

The sun went behind a cloud and the landscape darkened, the bright green of the grass fading to sage. The dry stone wall, which had been silvered by the sun, returned to its sombre dark hue. It was bitterly cold and, as the chill wind blew across the moor, Helena shivered. He did not seem to feel it, even when it blew his cloak open and whipped at the tails of his coat, for he stood there, motionless, making no move to fasten it.

At last he spoke.

'You asked me once how I earnt my name.'

She was very still, waiting for him to continue.

'I do not know why, but I have a mind to tell you.' He looked at the gravestone, as if he could see his brother's face there. 'It was on a dark night in the summer, when I had been to

161

a neighbour's ball. It had been a tedious evening, the conversation had been shallow and the company bored me. I left early, and returned to the castle. There was an . . . incident . . . ' He became lost in his thoughts, then seemed to rouse himself with difficulty. 'I knew at once that I had found my curse, or that my curse had found me. We are all cursed, we stormcrows. We are all fated to carry terrible news. It was my fate to carry it to my brother. I had to tell him that the woman he loved, his bride of a year, my sister-in-law, was dead.'

The wind moaned, and rain began to fall.

'I will never forget his face. I should have known better than to leave him. He went up to the battlements, his favourite place in times of sorrow — it had been so since he was a boy. He could barely see or think, driven mad by his grief.'

The wind howled.

'He fell from the battlements. I earnt my name not once, but twice: for then I had to carry the news of his death to my mother.'

'It was not your fault,' she said.

'No?' To her consternation he cupped her face, looking deeply into her eyes. 'I failed my brother, and I failed my sister-in-law. I will not fail again.'

His tone was sombre, and his words were

strange. She could not make sense of them, but she was finding it difficult to think clearly. Something about his touch confused her, blocking rational thought. Instead, she was a mass of feeling. She felt the wind; the wetness of the rain; the roughness of his skin against hers; the warmth of his breath on her face; and she began to tremble.

Each kiss a heart quake . . .

Byron's words came back to her.

And then, to her frustration, he lowered his hand and let her go. She had an impulse to take his hand and return it to her face, and it was only with an effort of will that she was able to resist. But she could not turn away from him.

What had happened? she asked herself, as she looked into his eyes. Why had he touched her? Why had he stroked her face? He was a strange man; secretive and haunted; but also a man of strong feelings, and a man who could arouse strong feelings in return.

Aloud, she said, 'I should return to the castle.'

'We will return together.'

He untethered his horse and they began to walk, and without willing it to be so, Helena found her steps coinciding with his. She felt wrapped around by an energy that encompassed them both, and for the first time in her life she knew she was not alone.

They walked on in silence, and she was seized by a strange thought, that it could be a thousand years in the past, or a thousand years in the future, and she would never know, for the moor was unchanging, a primitive landscape outside of time and place. She would not be surprised to see an elf or a hobgoblin walking across her path, some figure from folk tale long forgotten by civilization but remembered here, in the wilds, on an isolated pocket of land.

They walked in through the archway and the spell was broken, for there before them lay the castle, and in the courtyard, the maids were busy working. A groom came from the direction of the stables to take Lord Torkrow's horse. He relinquished the reins, and they went into the castle together. Once over the threshold, they heard the banter between the footmen and the maids who were washing the floor.

She was about to retire to the housekeeper's room when he said, 'I need to speak to you about the arrangement of the rooms for the ball.'

For a moment she thought it was a ruse, because he was finding it as hard to part from her as she was finding it to part from him, but his manner had returned to normal, and she quickly dismissed the idea.

'You will attend me in five minutes,' he said.

'Very well, my lord.'

She had time only to divest herself of her outdoor clothes before she went into the library, where he was waiting for her. The fire was dancing, the large flames licking the inner walls of the fireplace and filling the room with their crackling.

'The dancing will be held in the ballroom,' he said. 'It will need to be cleaned and polished. I will not have it disgracing the castle. The supper will be laid out in the dining-room. My overnight guests will dine with me at four o'clock, which will give you time to clear the room and arrange it for the ball before my other guests arrive.'

She had not expected him to take such a personal interest in the ball, but as there was no mistress of the house, she realized that he had no choice. He seemed to take no pleasure in it, but to regard it as a duty to his neighbours and a tribute to his ancestors.

'The ball will not finish until about three o'clock in the morning, but my overnight guests will require breakfast. Their servants will collect it from the kitchen, probably some time after midday.'

She listened as he told her of the castle

traditions, and she noted everything he said, but all the time she was thinking of his hand raised to her face and the feel of his skin on hers, and wondering what it would feel like if he kissed her.

'I will be going away for a few days, or possibly longer, but I will back before the ball,' he said at last.

'Very good, my lord,' she said, wondering where he was going.

He did not enlighten her, and she turned to go, but he said, 'I have not dismissed you.'

He sat down in a wing chair which was set on one side of the fire, and motioned her to sit in the other.

'I don't think I should sit,' she said.

'But I have chosen to do so, and as I have no intention of getting a stiff neck from looking up at you, you will oblige me,' he said.

She hesitated, then she smoothed her skirt beneath her and sat down on the edge of a chair.

'Do you need to take another book from the library, or are you still reading *Le Morte D'Arthur*?' he asked.

'I am still reading it, my lord. I have almost finished it — I read in the evenings when my work is done,' she added.

A ghost of a smile crossed his face. 'I was

not about to castigate you for neglecting your duties. I am glad you have had a chance to begin. I am interested to know what you think of it.'

'I am enjoying it. It is very pleasant to be spirited out of this world and into another for a time.'

'This world does not suit you?' he asked.

'It has its trials,' she said cautiously.

His reply was ironic. 'So it does. Very well. You like it for transporting you to another world. You do not find the tales realistic, then?'

She was surprised by the question, for the stories of knights and ladies, kings and queens, wizards and magic were far removed from reality.

'No,' she said.

'I think, perhaps, I do.' His shoulders sank, and his eyes turned in. 'Love is at the heart of the stories. Love of power. Love of men. Love of women. It is strange the things that love can do to a man, the journeys on which it can take him, the things it can make him feel and do. It is not a gentle thing, but a wild animal, without reason or pity; it rends and tears, making a mockery of goodness, destroying people. Love is a terrible thing.'

He fell silent, but was roused by a knocking at the door.

'Come!' he called.

Miss Parkins entered the room. She looked at Helena with hostility, and Helena felt her skin crawl, for she felt certain that Miss Parkins was her enemy. The woman's eyes might be dead, but Helena could feel her malice as a living thing.

'A letter has arrived by messenger, my lord. It has come from York.'

There was a sudden change in him; so sudden that Helena was shocked. His eyes flicked to hers, and it was as though a shutter had come down between them, breaking the bond that had been forming since their meeting in the graveyard.

'Thank you, Miss Parkins.' He turned to Helena, and said coldly, 'You have your instructions, Mrs Reynolds. You know all you need to know for the ball.'

'Very good, my lord.'

Helena rose, but as she left the room, she did not miss the look of malevolent triumph on Miss Parkins's face.

★ ★ ★

Simon waited only for the door to close, and then he broke the seal on the letter and read it.

'Well?' asked Miss Parkins.

'Mr Brunson has recovered and has returned to work,' he said. 'He is at my disposal. I think I will not see him here, it will seem odd, and I do not want anyone alerted to our suspicions. I will go to York instead. I will be able to get a description of Mrs Reynolds, and find out if she is the woman we have in the castle or not. I will go first thing tomorrow. And what of you? Have you discovered anything?'

'Nothing. She sent a letter to a friend, but it divulged very little.'

'You read it?'

'Of course, but I sealed it again afterwards.'

'And there was nothing incriminating?'

He saw her mind working behind her eyes.

'There was one strange sentence. She said she had not found what she was looking for, but did not despair of finding it.'

His expression darkened.

'It could mean she knows . . . ' — he shook his head — 'or it could mean nothing more than a lost shawl. Has she had a reply?'

'Yes. I did not manage to read it before she saw it.'

'A pity. Never mind. We must continue to be vigilant.'

Miss Parkins's look was derisory.

She knows I lowered my guard, he thought. I should not have done it. But there is something about Mrs Reynolds . . . if she is Mrs Reynolds, he reminded himself.

'Very good, Miss Parkins. That will be all.'

'Very good, my lord.'

As the door closed behind her, he walked over to the fire. His brother's death had been a terrible thing.

And his sister-in-law's death had been worse.

9

Helena was woken by the noise of hail pelting against the window and pulled the covers up over her ears. The sound was dispiriting; even more so when she shook away the last vestiges of sleep and remembered that it was Sunday, and that she had been hoping to go to church, so that she could talk to the villagers about her aunt. If the weather did not improve, that would be impossible, and she would have to remain in the castle, where she was in danger of being tangled up in the dark mysteries that hung about it, and even worse, where she was in danger of becoming attracted to Lord Torkrow.

In danger of becoming attracted to him? she thought, scoffing at herself. She was attracted to him already. There was no use denying her feelings, for they had undergone a change since arriving at the castle, turning from apprehension to intrigue, and then to something more.

It was compassion, she told herself firmly, nothing more than a kindly sympathy for a man who had had to carry the news of two deaths in one night. But it was no good. She knew it was not compassion, it was something much deeper.

She threw back the covers and climbed out of bed. At least the cold and the damp took her thoughts away from her other, more disturbing, subjects.

She washed and dressed quickly, then went downstairs to the kitchen. Over breakfast, Mrs Beal remarked that she would need more help in the kitchen as the ball approached, and she and Helena arranged for all the maids to spend a spell in the kitchen, so that Mrs Beal could choose the most useful girl to help her as the time drew near.

'The men will all have to learn how to carry a tray,' Mrs Beal reminded her.

Helena nodded, but her thoughts were less placid than her expression suggested. She knew she could not stay at the castle forever, and if not for the ball she would be thinking of leaving already, for she had explored almost every avenue of information open to her.

'And make sure they know how to behave,' said Mrs Beal. 'No talking to his lordship's guests. It's a good thing he's going away, it will make it easier for us to get on. We're lucky. He always sends word to the kitchen. He's a good master that way, though he can't say for sure when he'll be back. I expect he'll be gone for a few days, anyway.'

Helena did not know whether to be relieved or disappointed. He affected her in curious ways. He was secretive and alarming, but he moved her, too, and that was something no one else had ever done.

She finished her breakfast and then, leaving the kitchen behind her, she decided to revisit the east wing of the attic, in case she had missed anything. She found the door as she had left it. Ignoring the broken lock she went in, examining the blankets and pieces of broken furniture, then looking for other tell-tale signs that someone had been there. She breathed on the windows, remembering the times she and her aunt had written messages to each other in the steam when she had been a child, and recalling that once the steam had gone, the messages remained, to be revealed the next time the window misted over. But there was nothing.

She turned towards the door . . . and jumped, as she saw Miss Parkins standing there. She moves like a cat, thought Helena, unnerved by Miss Parkins's silent approach. Miss Parkins was standing with her hands folded in front of her and she looked at Helena with expressionless eyes.

'Miss Parkins,' said Helena, feeling that she

must speak. 'Did you want to see me about something?'

'I wanted to inform you that the door into the attic has been broken, but I see you have already discovered it,' said Miss Parkins, watching her. 'Do you know what happened?'

'Yes,' said Helena, standing up to her. 'One of the maids thought she heard a cat in here, and I ordered the footmen to break the lock. I was concerned that the animal might be trapped.'

'That is strange. Dawkins believed he heard a cat in there several weeks ago.'

'It must have crawled back in.'

Helena could tell that Miss Parkins did not believe her, but did not say so. Instead, it was as though they were playing some deadly game.

'And did you find it?' asked Miss Parkins.

'No. I believe it must have got out again without our help.'

'So there was no need to break the lock.'

'I did not know that at the time.' There was an awkward silence, then Helena said, 'I must not keep you.'

'You are not keeping me,' said Miss Parkins.

'Then you must excuse me. I have work to do.'

Miss Parkins did not move out of the way.

Instead she said, 'There was no mention of you destroying property in your previous positions.'

'I can see no point in discussing the matter further,' said Helena, unwilling to be drawn into a conversation about her supposed previous positions. 'If his lordship wishes to take the cost of repairing the lock from my wages, then I am sure he will do so.'

She did not ask Miss Parkins to leave again, she simply walked past her. She could feel Miss Parkins's eyes on her, but she resisted the urge to look back . . . until Miss Parkins spoke again, just as she reached the landing.

'I found a pile of handkerchiefs in the cupboard in your room,' she said. 'I expected to find them embroidered with your initials, ER, but instead they were embroidered with the initial C.'

Helena's throat constricted. She had forgotten to lock her door when she had gone downstairs for breakfast, and she was glad her back was to Miss Parkins, so that Miss Parkins would not see the consternation that swept across her face. Taking a moment to gather herself, she turned round and said, 'Do you make a habit of going into other people's rooms and going through their cupboards?'

'I feared it might be damp,' said Miss Parkins. 'I did not want your clothes to become mildewed.'

'It is not your job to see to damp cupboards. That is my preserve,' said Helena.

'I help his lordship in any way I can. Mrs Carlisle was also pleased to have my assistance. I am surprised you do not feel the same way. But you have not told me why your handkerchiefs bear the initial C.'

Helena had had time to think, and a simple solution to the problem had presented itself as her aunt's initial was also C.

'They are not my handkerchiefs. I found them in the cupboard. They must have belonged to the previous housekeeper.'

'How very singular,' said Miss Parkins, in a voice devoid of emotion.

'In what way?' asked Helena, suddenly apprehensive.

A malicious gleam of triumph entered Miss Parkins's eye.

'Mrs Carlisle did not occupy that room.'

Helena felt as though the floor had suddenly given way beneath her.

'I thought . . . that is, I assumed . . . that she had the bed chamber I now occupy.'

'No, she did not. So if she had had any handkerchiefs they would not have been in that room.'

'Perhaps she had just had them laundered,' said Helena, thinking quickly, 'and one of the maids returned them to the wrong room by mistake.'

'Strange that the maid should return them to a room with no fire, and no sheets on the bed,' said Miss Parkins.

Helena felt as though she was a mouse who had been caught by a particularly malignant cat.

'Perhaps she went into the room to air it, and then forgot to reclaim the handkerchiefs when she left,' Helena said.

'Mrs Carlisle was not a great believer in instructing the maids to air the rooms,' said Miss Parkins.

'Oh, yes — ' said Helena, about to say that her aunt had been a great believer in fresh air. She recovered herself quickly. 'She must have been. The room smelt fresh, not as though it had been shut up. Any good housekeeper knows the value of opening the windows when the weather is fine.'

Miss Parkins stared at her, and Helena felt an urge to squirm. She was held, mesmerized, by Miss Parkins's strange eyes, and she found herself wondering if she had ever seen Miss Parkins blink.

'Do you have a forwarding address? Then I can send them on to her,' said Helena, trying to turn the situation to her advantage.

'No. I have no address.'

'That is a pity. Then it seems I will have to keep them.'

'Perhaps you can use them yourself,' said Miss Parkins.

'I do not believe I would wish to do so,' said Helena, conscious of the fact that she had one such handkerchief tucked up her sleeve at that very moment. 'Now, Miss Parkins, I am very busy, and I will bid you good day.'

Helena turned and once more walked out on to the landing. As she did so, Miss Parkins said, 'The castle is a strange place. It has seen many strange things. No doubt, it will see many more.'

Helena did not look back, but felt uneasy as she went downstairs. Was it a threat? she wondered. Or was it a warning? Either way, she felt she must be on her guard.

★   ★   ★

Preparing the castle for the ball was hard work but, by and by, it began to take on a brighter air. The hall was clean and fresh, the downstairs rooms were dusted and the ballroom was ready. She and Mrs Beal were putting the finishing touches to the supper menu for the night of the ball.

'Of course, the balls aren't nearly as big as they were in her late ladyship's time. She had a lot of society friends and they came from all over: London, Edinburgh and Paris. Very good to the servants, she was, her ladyship. 'The servants must have their fun as well', she used to say. The day after the ball the family would be up late, and they'd have a bit of a sandwich for lunch. Then we'd lay out a cold supper for them in the dining-room at six o'clock and they'd help themselves. We had our own ball then, and didn't have to touch a bit of housework till the following morning ... A Solomon Grundy for the centre of the table?' she asked, breaking off in mid sentence to suggest a dish for the ball.

'Yes, that will look impressive,' said Helena.

Mrs Beal wrote it down.

'There were ever so many of us,' she said, reminiscing again. 'Mr Vance the butler — a very stately gentleman he was — kept everyone in order, and there were the outside staff, too, stable boys, grooms — and didn't they just chase the maids! — and coachmen, all dressed up.'

'The servants dressed up, too?' asked Helena, surprised.

'Yes. It was our own costume ball. Many a maid's been a queen on ball night. There were pirates and monks — Mr Vance was once Julius Caesar. 'Oh, Julius, seize her!' said one of the grooms, a cheeky young monkey, when Mr Vance was trying to pluck up the courage to dance with the housekeeper — I was just the kitchen maid then. Well, Mr Vance, he went bright red, but he did it all the same, seized her, that is, and the two of them whirled round the room. He married her in the end, and the two of them are living in Hull.

'We might get up some kind of dance on the night after the ball ourselves,' said Mrs Beal. 'Nothing so grand, but it might persuade the maids to stay if they think there's some fun to be had from time to time. I've still got the costumes, packed away in a tea chest.'

'I will speak to Lord Torkrow and see if he will allow it,' Helena said.

When they had agreed the final menu, she said, 'Where are the costumes? If his lordship approves of the ball, I will ask the maids to help me sort through them and see if they need washing or mending. They can choose what they will wear, and it will help me to encourage them to work hard. Some of them are prone to stop and gossip the minute my back is turned.'

'They're in the last pantry,' said Mrs Beal.

She took a key off a chain round her waist and handed it to Helena.

'I will go and make sure the moths haven't attacked them, before I mention it,' said Helena. 'Disappointed hopes will lead to less work, not more.'

Mrs Beal agreed.

'I've to go to the dairy, but you can give the key back to me when I return.'

Helena took the key and went through the first pantry and into a smaller one. After going through five similar rooms, each with its own purpose, she came to one that was empty apart from a large tea chest. She knelt down and opened the chest. There was a musty smell as she lifted the lid, but she saw that the costumes were in good condition. She took out a medieval gown made of dark red velvet. Beneath it was a gold mask. She picked it up and an idea came to her. If she wore it on the night of the ball, then she could pass unnoticed amongst Lord Torkrow's guests. She had been getting nowhere in her quest to find her aunt, but if she could talk to the neighbouring gentry she might learn something. She had been hoping she might overhear something of use at the ball, but, as a guest, she could ask questions.

One of them might have seen her aunt board the stagecoach if they had been returning home after a night of carousing, and she might learn, at least, if her aunt had gone north or south.

She closed the chest, resolving to return and take the medieval gown up to her room later, together with the hat, mask and shoes that went with it. If she mixed them in with a pile of freshly laundered sheets, then no one would see what she was doing.

As she stood up, she noticed that a small door led out of the pantry, opposite the door through which she had come. It was only two and a half feet high, and she was curious as to its purpose. She tried the handle, and the door opened. It led into a low passageway. It was dark inside. She looked around the pantry, finding a candle and tinder box in a drawer. Lighting the candle, she knelt down and peered into the tunnel. It smelled dank. The floor was made of hard-packed earth, and as she put out her hand to feel it, she discovered it was damp. She did not want to go through, but she could not ignore what she had found, so, pushing the candle in front of her, she began to crawl through the tunnel. She felt the damp seeping through her dress, and her knees were cold. She looked over her shoulder, wondering if she should close the door, for it would look strange if anyone entered the room, but she had a fear of being shut in. Besides, the light was a help, both to her eyes and her nerves.

She went on, shivering as the dank walls closed about her and watching the candle flame anxiously as it flickered and spurted in the gloom.

She had not gone far, however, when the roof began to rise, and before long she could stand up. She walked for some distance before she found her way blocked by another door. She tried to open it, but it was heavy, and it was not until she set her shoulder to it that she felt it give. She pushed with all her might and slowly it opened. She went through and found herself in a mausoleum. The desolate place made her shiver, and the candle flickered with the trembling of her hand. In the corners of the stone edifice were leaf skeletons, dry and brittle and decayed with age. Dust lay thickly on the floor, and spiders' webs hung from the stone ceiling. In the centre of the mausoleum was a tomb. Helena went forward and examined it. The stone figure of a man lay on the tomb with his feet on a lion. He was dressed in stone armour and a stone sword was at his side. He was, Helena guessed, one of Lord Torkrow's ancestors.

As she lifted the candle higher, her eye was caught by something odd in the far corner.

She moved forward to see it better. It was a bare patch on the floor, where the dust had been swept clean. Someone had been there recently. Lovers, she wondered, seeking a place of solitude? Or someone else?

She brushed the floor with her hand, hoping to find some clue: a plaited piece of dried lavender, perhaps, or a brooch; but there was nothing. She stood up and went over to the main door. It opened inwards, and, with difficulty, she managed to pull it towards her. The daylight hurt her eyes. The sun had come out and, after the darkness of the tunnel and the mausoleum, it seemed dazzling. She blinked several times, then, loath to return to the dank tunnel, she blew out her candle, closed the door, and set off across the moor.

It was a beautiful day. The weather was unseasonably warm, and there was a strength in the sunshine that reminded her that spring was just around the corner. The sky above her was blue, and the breeze blew a few wispy white clouds across it. The grass beneath her feet was springy, and was enlivened with bright patches of heather. Red and purple tried to out do each other with their vivid display.

On such a beautiful day the moor looked peaceful, not a brooding enemy, but a friend.

Far off, the castle basked in the sunshine, its stone appearing mellow in the light. Even the crenellations seemed less threatening, reminding her of the gimping on the edges of Mrs Beal's pastry instead of broken teeth.

It seemed impossible to think that any evil had befallen her aunt. But if not, where could she be? Could she have gone away for a holiday? Or could she, perhaps, have been lured away from the castle with an offer of a higher salary? But then why would she lie to Lord Torkrow about it?

The more Helena thought about it, the less her aunt's disappearance made sense. But it had happened, and perhaps, at the ball, she would have a chance to find out something more.

As she approached the castle, she wondered if the maids would have taken advantage of her absence, but there was a flurry of activity when she went into the castle, and she was pleased to see that everyone was working.

'We're going to be short of chairs,' said Manners, one of the footmen, coming up to her.

Manners had been at the castle the last time a costume ball had been held, and he had been a great help with the preparations.

'What did you do last year?' asked Helena.

'Brung some down from the attic.'

'Then that is what we will do this year,' said Helena.

'Yes, missus.'

'Is there anything else we need from the attic?'

'There's a trestle table up there. It needs its leg fixing, but then it'll be good as new.'

'See to it, Manners, if you please.'

'Yes, missus.'

'I will leave you to organize it.'

He nodded, and went away, calling for two of the other men to help him. She left them to their task, and, seeing Effie going into the housekeeper's room to mend the fire, she went down to the kitchen again. Mrs Beal had not returned from the dairy and, going into the pantry, she put the candle back in its place and closed the door into the tunnel. She laid the medieval costume on top of the tea chest, then collected some sheets from the laundry. Concealing the costume in the pile of linen, she made her way up to her chamber.

She was about to put the costume in her wardrobe when she remembered that Miss Parkins had been through her things once before. She did not want to take the chance of the maid finding her costume if she should happen to forget to lock her door again. She thought for a few minutes, and then she went into one of the disused bedchambers at the end of the corridor. She took the precaution of placing a chair in front of the door and then she relaxed.

She looked about her. The room was almost bare. There was a dusty cheval glass and a wardrobe. There was also a bed, but it had no sheets on it and the mattress was tattered. The grate was empty, and from the look of it there had not been a fire there for a long time. The mantelpiece was chipped and the wallpaper was hanging from the walls.

As she had already apportioned the rooms for Lord Torkrow's overnight guests, she knew it would not be needed on the night of the ball, which was fortunate, as it was not a room anyone would wish to use. It would be perfect for her purposes.

She went over to the wardrobe and examined it. Outside, it was dusty, but inside, the shelves were clean. There was an old straw hat and a fan inside, and on the bottom shelf there was a blanket, but nothing else. She was about to put her costume inside when she was overcome with a strong urge to try it on. Quickly, she stripped off her woollen gown and petticoats, shivering in the cold air as she was left standing in her chemise and drawers.

She picked up the medieval dress and

dropped it over her head. The velvet slipped over her skin, and she felt a sensuous pleasure at the feel of the fabric as it slid over her arms, down over her chest and then fell in folds around her legs and feet. She had never worn a dress like this before, and she ran her hands over it, revelling in the feel of the velvet. The pile was deep, and she stroked it both ways, enjoying the contrast between the rough and the smooth sensations. It was so different from the thick woollen gowns she usually wore, and the feel of it against her skin was luxurious.

She turned round to pick up the wig, and stood transfixed as she saw herself in the cheval glass. Gone was her dumpy figure, padded out by layers of petticoats and a thick woollen gown. In its place was a willowiness she had not suspected. The simple lines of the dress followed the contours of her body. The rich red accentuated her smooth cream skin, and gave more colour to her lips.

She put on the wig, and she could hardly believe that the person in the mirror was her. The dark wig made her eyes seem deeper set, and the style changed the shape of her face from a heart to an oval. She put on the tall, pointed hat and the transformation was complete. No one who did not know her well would suspect who she was, and with a mask the disguise would be impenetrable.

She felt things were coming to a head. She would ask as many questions as she could at the ball, and she had a sense that some of them might be answered. At last, she would learn some clue to her aunt's whereabouts and strange disappearance.

She was loath to remove the costume, with its rich colours and its sensuous feel, but she did not want to be away from the other servants for too long, for she did not want anyone asking awkward questions about where she had been, so she changed quickly, then hid the costume under the blanket at the bottom of the wardrobe. She dressed in her own clothes then removed the chair from in front of the door. She listened, making sure no one was coming along the landing, then she went out, and was soon downstairs.

'Did you find everything you needed?' she asked Manners, as she saw him standing by a line of chairs.

'Yes, it was all there,' he said. 'I've had a look at the table, and I can mend the leg. I'll have it done by tomorrow.'

'Good.'

She went into the ballroom. The dust sheets had gone and the floor had been swept. The *bobéches* for the chandelier had been washed, and two of the maids were putting them back in place, so that they would catch the hot wax that fell from the candles. Chairs had been arranged down either side of the room, and the mirrors had been polished.

'This is looking very well,' she said to the maids. 'You've worked hard.'

It seemed that the preparations for the ball might be finished on time, after all.

* * *

Simon, Lord Torkrow, returned to the castle, weary from his journey, and weary, too, from the waste of his time. As he rode into the courtyard, he thought of his unsuccessful interview with Mr Brunson, whose description of Mrs Reynolds had been so vague as to be worthless. *A very pleasant widow, of medium build . . . medium height . . . brown hair . . . possibly twenty-five or thirty-five years of age . . .*

He was reluctant to dismount as his horse came to a halt. He had been glad to be away from the castle, for he had been thinking more and more about his housekeeper, which was foolish, when he did not know who she was, and disastrous, when he recalled the pain of love. It was not an emotion to be welcomed; it was one to be fought.

190

A groom came out to meet him and he could delay no longer. He dismounted and went inside. He saw Mrs Reynolds as he crossed the hall, and although he was loath to speak to her he knew he must, for there were some details he needed to arrange for the ball.

'Mrs Reynolds, a word, if you please.'

She joined him in the library, standing before him with hands folded, perfectly poised. Was she who she claimed to be? He could not believe any evil of her. And yet he could not be sure. She asked too many questions, and wanted to know too much.

'I want to speak to you about the final arrangements for the ball,' he said.

'Yes, my lord.'

'Tell me, will everything be ready on time?'

'Yes, my lord.'

'Good.' He had no desire to hold a ball, but now that he was doing so, he expected everything to go well. The castle had a long tradition to uphold, for the balls in his parents' time were spoken of far and wide, and he was determined that this year's ball should not be an exception.

'Here is the final list of overnight guests.'

He handed it to her, and she looked at it

'The Harcourts will be arriving early. They have a long way to come, and as Mrs

Harcourt does not travel well, she prefers to arrive well in advance. I have made a note of those people who should have rooms together and those who should not under any circumstances be in the same wing. It is unfortunately necessary for me to invite my family, many of whom dislike each other, but I do not intend to compound the problem by housing them too close to each other.'

'I will make sure they are accommodated as you desire.'

'Is there anything else you need to help you?' he asked.

'No, thank you.' She hesitated, then said, 'There is just one thing, my lord.'

'Well?' he asked.

'Mrs Beal tells me that the staff used to be able to hold their own costume ball on the evening after the castle ball. If you are agreeable, I would like to revive the custom.'

He was thoughtful, as he recalled the custom.

'It will be a way of thanking the servants for their hard work,' said Helena.

'I remember . . . yes, very well, Mrs Reynolds, as long as they do not begin their celebrations until after my last guest has been attended to. See to it.'

'Thank you, my lord.'

Helena returned to the sitting-room and

found the maids were lifting the rugs.

'Don't know why we 'ave to lift the rugs,' said Sally.

'The colours will be much brighter when you have beaten them,' said Helena.

'It's a powerful lot of work,' grumbled Martha.

'Yes, it is, but once it is done the room will look much more cared for.'

'All right for some folks who 'as balls to go to,' muttered Sally, under her breath. 'It's others who 'ave to do all the work.'

'But when all the work is done, and the ball is over, then we will have our own ball,' said Helena.

The girls looked up hopefully.

'His lordship has given me permission to revive the servants' costume ball. Once you have finished your work, you may go down to the pantry and choose a costume from the tea chest. But the rugs must be beaten first, and beaten well.'

'Yes, missus, it will be,' said the girls.

They set to work with renewed vigour. They took the rugs outside and hit them with all their might, sending clouds of dust spiralling into the early spring sunshine.

10

It was fortunate the previous weeks had been fine, thought Helena, as she oversaw the last minute preparations for the ball. It had allowed the maids to beat the carpets, wash the curtains, and air the rooms. She had been so busy that her worries about her aunt had been pushed to the back of her mind, to resurface in quiet moments. If she did not learn anything at the ball — she did not allow herself to think of it: she *would* learn something at the ball.

She turned her attention back to her work. There would be few flowers to decorate the castle, but there were plenty of other things to brighten the April gloom. Huge fires were lit in every room, and the reds and oranges of the flames cast a rosy glow over the walls and furniture. The carpets, newly beaten, were colourful, and she had brought more paintings down from the attic. Some had needed their frames mending and some had needed restringing, but all now adorned the walls. There were portraits, hunting scenes and beautiful views of the castle, painted in the summer, which brought the promise of blue skies and sunshine to the rooms.

She went down into the kitchen to see how Mrs Beal was getting along. The cook was directing the women and girls who had been hired to help her, and the kitchen was a mass of loaves, cakes and other tempting food. Joints of meat were roasting over the spit, and pies and pasties were being filled with sweet and savoury fillings. The room was warm, and full of all the varied scents of cooking: the smell of meat mixed with the smell of herbs and spices to create a heady brew.

Helena went into the pantry, where the cool marble surfaces displayed a collection of cheese, butter, milk, eggs and cream.

Satisfied that Mrs Beal had everything well in hand, she paused only to offer a few words of encouragement and then went to the housekeeper's room. She was about to go in when she saw Lord Torkrow crossing the hall. He was looking about him, taking an interest in everything that had been done.

'You have done well,' he said to her. 'I have never seen the castle looking better.'

'Thank you.'

'Now, to business. I will greet my guests as they arrive, and you will escort them to their rooms.'

'Very good, my lord.'

'I will be glad when this evening is over,' he

said, looking around once more, and speaking as though he had forgotten she was there. 'If the company were more congenial and the chatter not so inconsequential, then perhaps . . . But there is not one single person I wish to see and I have a horror of playing the charming host to people I despise.'

Helena's feelings were written across her face.

'You think I will not play the charming host?' he asked. 'Perhaps you are right. My charm has long since deserted me.'

He continued on his way. As Helena went into the housekeeper's room, she found herself wondering what he would say if he knew that there was going to be an unexpected guest at the ball, and that she would be the lady in medieval costume.

★   ★   ★

The first guests, Mr and Mrs Harcourt, arrived at midday. Lord Torkrow greeted them with civility if not warmth, and Helena conducted them to their room. They did not seem a happy couple, despite their evident wealth. Mr Harcourt was a man approaching forty years of age, with features that had once been handsome but were now growing slack with dissipation. His breath smelled of brandy, though the hour was early, and there was a restless look in his eye. His clothes were impeccably cut, but the collar and cuffs showed signs of fraying, indicating that he had seen better times. He wore no jewellery save a signet ring on one finger, and paid no attention to his wife, although without her he would not have been invited, for it was his wife who was a cousin of Lord Torkrow.

Mrs Harcourt herself had an ill-humoured look. She, too, was dressed in expensive clothes that had seen better days. She set about abusing her maid, an elderly, tired-looking woman, before declaring she had a headache and commanding Helena to send her an infusion of camomile at once.

'Of course,' said Helena.

As she left the room, Mr Harcourt cast a speculative glance in her direction.

'Don't send any of the girls up to Mr and Mrs Harcourt's room,' she warned Mrs Beal, as she entered the kitchen and set about making the tea.

'I wouldn't think of it,' said Mrs Beal with a snort. 'We've had Mr Harcourt here before. Mrs Carlisle had her work cut out for her, keeping him away from the maids.'

Helena pitied her aunt, knowing it could not have been easy. Her aunt would have been polite but strong and Mr Harcourt . . . her thoughts stopped. What would Mr Harcourt have done if her aunt had crossed him?

'When was Mr Harcourt last here?' she asked.

'Not for a long time, at least not to stay. He visits the castle from time to time on county business, but his lordship won't have him here overnight if it can be helped.'

Helena dropped a handful of camomile flowers in the pot and poured the water on to them.

'And when did he last come on business?' she asked.

'I don't know. I don't see him come and go. I'm down in my kitchen, and glad of it. Dawkins shows him in and out.'

Helena resolved to speak to Dawkins about it when she had a chance. If Mr Harcourt had been at the castle on the day of her aunt's disappearance, perhaps he had had something to do with it.

'Are there any more guests I need to be wary of?' asked Helena, as she set a cup and saucer on a tray.

'Stay away from Lady Jassry. She's a tongue as sharp as my kitchen knife, and Mrs Yorke will likely accuse you of stealing her jewels if you go in her room. But the others are mostly well behaved.'

Helena gave the tray to the oldest village woman, a stoutly made matron of ample girth, and told her to carry it upstairs.

She was kept busy throughout the afternoon as carriages rolled up at the door, spilling out their guests. They were elegant and well dressed, and were accompanied by valets and maids, who hastened to do everything to ensure the comfort of their masters and mistresses, whilst managing to banter between themselves.

Helena was kept busy showing guests to their rooms and making sure that the servants knew where they were to eat and sleep. Many had been to the castle before, but for some it was their first time, and twice Helena came across tearful maids who were lost in the castle's corridors.

Mrs Beal was like three women, seeing to the roasting and boiling of meats, overseeing the preparation of mountains of vegetables, putting the finishing touches to the pies and puddings that had already been made, and were in the pantry, ready for their grand entrance at the end of dinner. She chivvied the maids who were making the tea and checked each tray before it left the kitchen, making sure there was a good selection of cakes and biscuits to go to each room.

The musicians arrived. They knew where to go, having played at the castle before, and they established themselves in the minstrels' gallery, tuning their instruments before trying out a variety of tunes.

The holiday atmosphere was infectious, and for the first time Helena saw the castle as it must have been when Lord Torkrow's parents were still alive. Every downstairs room was open, and every bedroom in the west wing. The dust sheets had gone and the fires had been lit. The candelabras were set in front of polished mirrors that reflected the dancing light.

At last, the overnight guests had all arrived, and were safely in their rooms. Helena retired to the kitchen, where she and Mrs Beal had a sandwich and a slice of pie before turning their attention to preparing dinner for Lord Torkrow's guests.

'I'll be glad when dinner's over,' said Mrs Beal. 'Then we can get on with laying out supper in the dining-room.'

Four o'clock arrived, and dinner was served to Lord Torkrow and his guests. Mrs Beal waited impatiently for them to finish, and as soon as they had left the dining-room and retired to their bedchambers to prepare for the ball, she began to organize the maids and footmen, who quickly cleared dinner and then started carrying the less delicate supper foods upstairs.

At seven o'clock, Helena paused for breath, looking over the groaning tables. The white damask cloths could barely be seen beneath silver platters, candelabras and crystal bowls on tall stems containing pyramids of fruit.

At ten minutes to eight, Lord Torkrow appeared in the hall. He was dressed in a black tailcoat with black pantaloons.

'Is everything ready?' he asked Helena, as she hurried through the hall.

'Yes, my lord.'

The sound of a carriage crunching on the gravel outside could be heard. Helena glanced to the door. Dawkins was there, dressed in his best livery, ready to open it. Helena had taken the precaution of locking the door to the west wing of the attic so that he could not get on to the battlements, and if he had noticed, he had not said so. Indeed, how could he mention it, without revealing that he had a reason for wanting to go there? The ruse had kept him sober and, as a loud knock came at the door, he opened it with aplomb.

It was the Fairdeans who had arrived. Helena showed them to the ladies' withdrawing-room, where their maid helped them to remove their cloaks. Miss Fairdean looked exquisite in a daring costume proclaiming her to be a wood nymph. The diaphanous material of her gown was skilfully woven in different shades of blue and green which changed with the light, giving a magical impression. She preened herself in front of the mirror, ignoring Helena in the way she ignored the chairs and washstand, whilst her maid and her mother both flattered her.

Helena followed them out of the room, whereupon they sought out Lord Torkrow, congratulating him on the splendour of the castle — 'a magnificent sight'; his attire — 'so clever of you to resist the urge to dress up, I'm sure the rest of us must seem like children to you'; and his goodness in holding the ball — 'for it must be quite a burden to you, but all your friends do so enjoy it'.

Helena saw his look of contempt, and thought that Miss Fairdean should say less if she wanted to attract him more.

Helena was kept busy as more and more guests arrived. Footmen hurried past her, carrying trays of wine, the musicians played lively airs, and the ballroom began to fill with dancers.

When all the guests had arrived, Helena allowed herself a few quiet minutes in the housekeeper's room, glad of the forethought that had led her to place a tray there so that she could refresh herself before proceeding with her plan.

It was still not too late to abandon the idea. If her masquerade was discovered, she could find herself in danger. But if not, she could learn something useful.

She had a small glass of ratafia and several biscuits. Her energy renewed, she was about to go upstairs to change when the door opened and Mr Harcourt entered. He was dressed as Don Juan, with a short black cloak over black trousers and white shirt, and on his head he wore a black hat. Strings dangled from it, falling loosely beneath his chin. His eyes were covered with a black mask, but Helena recognized him by the ring on his finger and the smell of brandy on his breath.

'I've been waiting for this moment all evening,' he said. 'I thought I'd never get you alone, and then I saw you slipping in here. All you seem to do is work. That doesn't seem fair, when everyone else is enjoying the ball.'

'It is my job,' said Helena.

'It doesn't have to be,' he said, sitting down on a corner of the desk, with one foot touching the floor and one foot left dangling. He leant forwards in a familiar way. 'There are better ways to earn a living. Easier, too. No more lighting fires and cleaning grates.'

'I am a housekeeper. I do not light fires or

clean grates,' she told him coolly. 'Now, if you will excuse me, I am just on my way to the ballroom.'

He stood up and blocked her path.

'It's a pity to see such a young woman wearing such an old gown,' he said, stroking her shoulder. 'And a pretty woman, too. Such beautiful hair . . . so rich and thick . . . It could be properly dressed, if you had a little money to play with.'

'Is this the way you always behave with housekeepers?' she demanded, as she shrugged away from him. 'Did you insult Mrs Carlisle in this way too?'

'Mrs Carlisle?'

'His lordship's previous housekeeper.'

He laughed.

'I'd have had to be desperate to do that. The women was old and sour, and fit for nothing but drudgery. But you — '

'Enough,' said Helena.

She attempted to side step past him, but he stepped to the side as well.

'Why so hasty? I have a proposition to put to you, one that would be worth you listening to. You don't have to go around in old rags, you could have something new and pretty to wear.' He plucked at the sleeve of her thick woollen gown. 'Not something coarse like this, but something made of silk, or satin.

Something bright, like a butterfly. You could have jewels at your throat and a bracelet on your wrist.'

He stroked her arm as he said it. She shuddered, and pulled it away.

'I am satisfied with what I have,' she said quellingly.

'Oh, no, not *satisfied*. You don't know what it is to be *satisfied*,' he said suggestively. 'But I can teach you. You'd be a good student, I'll be bound.'

'I must go,' said Helena. 'I am needed to give instructions to the maids. I will be missed.'

'Not for a few minutes you won't, and a few minutes is all it takes for you to earn a golden guinea.'

He took one out of his pocket and held it up in front of her.

She was enraged. It was bad enough that he should think the sight of gold would dazzle her and it was a hundred times worse that he should think one guinea should suffice to buy her. The final insult was that he would think she would earn money in that way in the first place.

'Get out of my way,' she said, all politeness gone.

'So you're a woman of passion,' he said, bending forward to whisper in her ear. His breath was hot and wet and made her shudder. 'I like that. But I can teach you how to channel that passion in other, more exciting ways, and I can teach you how to earn money from it as well. There's a guinea for you now, and another one when you come to my room tonight. Or would you rather have a lesson here?'

She pushed past him and ran into the hall, losing herself quickly in the crowd of guests. She glanced in the mirror hanging on the wall and saw no sign of him having followed her, so she put the incident behind her and went upstairs. She made her way to the empty bedchamber and then closed and locked the door behind her. She was suddenly nervous. If she went through with her plan — if she dressed up and went to the ball — then she would probably lose her position if she was discovered. But if she did not, then she might never find out what had happened to her aunt.

She slipped off her dress, feeling the cold bite of the air as her limbs were exposed. She almost wished she had ordered a fire lit in the room, but no, it was better this way, for with its abandoned air, the room had not attracted any unwelcome guests; young ladies retreating from the noise, or couples keeping secret assignations.

Quickly she took off her petticoats and donned the red velvet dress. As it whispered down over skin, she felt herself taking on a new persona, and as she put on the wig and fastened the mask over her eyes she thought to herself that it was a disguise within a disguise: the medieval lady was a disguise for Mrs Reynolds, and Elizabeth Reynolds was a disguise for Helena Carlisle. She put on a pair of shoes with red high heels that had been in the tea chest with the dress, and then put on the hat.

Even Aunt Hester would not know me now, she thought.

She opened the door and the sound of music became louder. Voices rose up from below, chattering and laughing. She went along the corridor and down the stairs, keeping to the shadows so as not to draw attention to herself. As she descended, she cast her eyes over all the people. Kings and queens, monks and fairies, knights and ladies all mingled together, filling the sombre castle with their brilliance. Masks covered their faces, some no larger than was necessary to cover their eyes, some obscuring their entire heads.

Everywhere she looked she saw illusion, as people pretended to be something they were not. And then she saw Lord Torkrow, black against the dazzling background. He disdained pretence, and proclaimed to the world who he was. His face was unmasked. He was something real and solid in the sea of disguise. His strong features were shown off by the candlelight, and it created light and shade in patterns across his face. It was like his character, she thought, a perplexing mix of light and shade.

'Champagne?' came a respectful voice at her side.

It was Dawkins. She stiffened, afraid he might recognize her, but his face was impassive. She took a glass and he moved on. She felt her confidence grow. She moved through the room with ease, as though it was her right to be there, sipping her champagne. But her new-found security vanished when, going into the ballroom some five minutes later, she saw Lord Torkrow walking towards her. He was not looking at her, though, and after briefly faltering she continued, but as she drew level with him, his eyes flicked to hers, and she knew a moment of panic. Her pulse escalated still further when he stopped and looked at her curiously, as if trying to remember where he had seen her before. Then he said, 'May I have the pleasure of this dance?'

She searched her mind for an excuse, but

before she could think of one he had taken her hand and led her on to the floor.

There was a stir of interest around them. The opening chords of the dance sounded, and Helena swept a curtsy. The dress made the action extravagant, and she was beginning to find the evening stimulating. She had never been to a ball before, and the sounds and scents were intoxicating.

Opposite her, Lord Torkrow bowed. She seemed to be seeing him more clearly than usual, as though the stimulation of her other senses had stimulated her sight as well. The deepset eyes, the high cheekbones, the pointed chin all drew her eye. He was not handsome, and yet she found his features strangely compelling, and her gaze roved over his face, taking it in.

They began to dance. As they walked towards each other, Helena felt a shiver of anticipation as their hands touched each other in a star. They separated, and she found herself looking forward to the next contact. They repeated the measure, and came together again.

'I don't believe I know you,' said Lord Torkrow, looking at her curiously.

Helena did not reply.

'Are you a friend of Miss Cartwright's?'

She smiled and shook her head.

'Then a cousin of Mr Kerson's?'

Again she shook her head.

The dance parted them, and she was relieved to be away from him. So far, she had answered all his questions with a nod or a shake of the head, but there would be other questions, more difficult to answer.

When they came together again, he asked, 'Will you be staying in the neighbourhood long?'

She shook her head.

'Do you never speak?' he asked, his voice intrigued.

She shook her head again.

'*Can* you speak?'

She felt a vibration in the air, as though the very effort to hold him away from her was setting up a resonance in the atmosphere. He seemed to feel it too. The music faded into the background and the chatter died away. She forgot the other dancers existed. She was aware of only the two of them, and everything else was a blur. She saw that his eyes were not brown as she had thought, but were flecked with different colours, gold and green, and his lashes were long and thick. She was aware of his scent, deep and masculine, and she shivered every time he took her hand, for there were no gloves with her costume, nor did he wear them, and the feel of his skin on hers was exhilarating. The music came to an end, but she was scarcely aware of it, and remained standing opposite him, connected to him by an invisible thread.

It was only when a dowager bumped into her that she was recalled to her surroundings, and felt as though she had awakened from a dream. The chatter returned, and the people, and she was once more in the ballroom with all the guests.

She remembered why she had entered into the masquerade, reminding herself that, once she had found out what had happened to her aunt, she would have to leave the castle, and she was conscious of a strange reluctance to discover the truth.

'This is a wonderful ball,' came a voice she recognized, and she found that Miss Fairdean had joined them. Miss Fairdean had placed herself between Helena and Lord Torkrow, and, recalled to her senses, Helena took the opportunity to slip away. She went into the supper room, feeling disquieted, and still feeling the after effects of the dance as, in the early mornings, she remembered the lingering traces of her dreams.

She shook her head, in an effort to shake it away.

She found herself standing next to a gentleman dressed in a brightly-coloured harlequin's costume. It was made from diamonds of red, yellow and blue cloth, and it had a matching mask, with a red diamond over his left eye and a yellow diamond over his right.

'Good evening, Harlequin,' said a woman dressed in a gown of white feathers.

'Evening, Mistress Swan,' he said. 'Or should I say Mrs Cranfield?'

She fluttered her fan and giggled.

Then his eyes drifted to Helena. 'And who are you, m' beauty?' he asked, as he turned to look at her.

Despite his juicy relish in calling her 'm'beauty', Helena sensed no harm in him and replied laughingly, 'I am not allowed to tell.'

'Ah! I've caught you out, Miss Garson,' he said, as he took a bite of a chicken leg.

'Not Miss Garson,' said another gentleman close by. 'Miss Garson's dressed as the Queen of Sheba. I saw her earlier.'

'Not Miss Garson?' said the Harlequin.

'No, sir, and please, don't guess any further,' said Helena.

'All will be revealed at midnight, eh?' he said.

'It will,' she agreed. 'Until then, we must enjoy ourselves. The castle is looking splendid. When his lordship's housekeeper disappeared, I feared his lordship would not go ahead with the ball.'

'That'd have been a pity. I wouldn't be here, talking to you, now, would I?'

'Do you know what happened to her?' asked Helena.

'Who? Miss Garson?' he asked, with another chicken leg halfway to his mouth.

'No. His lordship's housekeeper.'

'His lordship's housekeeper?' he said with a roar of laughter. 'How should I know? I don't keep a watch on his servants, m'pretty!'

'I was hoping to employ her,' said a woman standing next to him, who was dressed as a milkmaid. Her hat was askew and her dress was bunched up at one side. 'If she can keep a castle clean, she can manage my manor. You cannot imagine how hard it is to find good servants. My last housekeeper left after a week, saying the moors preyed on her nerves. I said to her: 'They prey on all our nerves, but we don't give in to it. We stiffen our backbones.' But it was no good. She didn't listen. Said she wanted to go back to Nottingham and left the following morning. No staying power, that's what's wrong with servants these days.'

'Do you know where his lordship's housekeeper went?' asked Helena.

'I wish I did. I can't ask his lordship, I

don't want him to think I'm the sort of woman who goes about taking other people's servants. But if I find out, I will offer her double her present wage to come to me.'

'That's the spirit!' said Harlequin.

'Sir Hugh Greer? Is that you?' asked the milkmaid, peering at him.

'Give us a kiss and I'll tell you!' he said.

'It is you!' she said. 'I thought I recognized the voice. Such behaviour from a justice of the peace.'

'Not a justice tonight,' he said jovially. 'I'm Harlequin, and Harlequin doesn't deal with trouble, he makes it!'

He lunged good-naturedly at the milkmaid, who picked up her skirts and, with a whoop of laughter, ran off into the crowd, pursued by Sir Hugh.

Helena was about to move on when she heard a voice at her shoulder and froze as she realized Lord Torkrow had found her.

'If I didn't know better, I would think you were running away from me,' he said.

She could not avoid speaking to him for ever, but she hoped that the noise of the room would disguise her voice. Even so, she deliberately pitched it lower than usual.

'Perhaps I was,' she said.

'Are you afraid of me?' he asked, his eyes looking into her face as though he could see

214

through the mask and discover her identity.

'No,' she replied.

'Then you are unusual,' he said. 'Everyone else here is.'

'Miss Fairdean doesn't seem to be afraid of you,' she remarked.

The mask had given her courage, and she found she could say things to him that would have been unthinkable in her housekeeper's clothes.

He raised his eyebrows, but replied, 'You are wrong. She is. But she is also avaricious and she fancies herself as the mistress of a castle, so she hides her fear deep. If she ever found herself alone with me, she would repent her bargain. Whereas you . . . '

' . . . have my reputation to protect, and would never be alone with a gentleman,' she said.

'No?' he asked. His eyes glittered, and she felt her own widen in response.

'No,' she said, though her breathing became shallow.

'Perhaps you are wise. Temptation is a terrible thing. But you're not eating,' he said, abruptly changing the conversation.

He took a plate and began to put some of the choicest food on it.

'I am not hungry,' she said.

'You must have something. I am your host.

I insist. Try a sugared almond. They are very good.'

He picked one up and held it up to her lips. She took it into her mouth, tasting the sweet sugar and the nutty flavour, and alongside it she tasted the saltiness of his skin. She had an almost overwhelming urge to taste more, but she jerked her head away before she could give in to temptation.

'I am looking forward to midnight,' he said softly.

Helena thought with relief, I will not be here at midnight. When the rest of the guests unmask, I will be safely in the kitchen, dressed in my housekeeper's clothes.

'My lord, at last!' came a voice at their side. 'I have been looking for you everywhere. I am sure you remember that I promised to introduce you to my niece when last we met. Talia, make your curtsy to his lordship. She is staying with us for a while, your lordship, and we are very glad to have her with us. Such a good girl! Such pretty manners. Now, now, child, don't blush.'

The poor young girl had gone scarlet, and was looking at Lord Torkrow with a mixture of fear and awe.

He replied politely. 'Miss Winson. It is good of you to come. I hope you are enjoying your first costume ball.'

216

As the girl mumbled a reply, Helena slipped away and went into the ballroom. A young man dressed as a knight asked for her hand and led her to safety out on to the floor. She began to talk of the splendour of the castle and mentioned Mrs Carlisle, but her partner could shed no light on Mrs Carlisle's disappearance. He was far more interested in trying to discover Helena's identity. Helena parried his questions easily, but she did not learn anything of use.

She went out into the hall when the dance was over, hoping that she would learn more from his lordship's female guests. They might have heard something from their own servants, or have made enquiries if they wanted to hire Mrs Carlisle themselves.

'Lord Torkrow will never marry her,' she heard a young woman saying. The young woman had a clumsy build, and was dressed unbecomingly as Joan of Arc. 'She's been setting her cap at his lordship for the last three years, but he's never so much as looked at her. I cannot think why she wants to attract him. He makes me shiver. There's something in his eyes — he's a cold man.'

No, thought Helena, remembering the flash in his eye as he had fed her the almond. He's far from cold.

'He wasn't so cold with his sister-in-law,'

said another woman who was dressed as Maid Marion.

'Sh,' said the Amazon next to her.

'Why?' asked Maid Marion belligerently. 'I'm only saying what everyone knows.'

'I don't know it,' said a young woman dressed as a Greek goddess.

'Better not say anything more,' said Nell Gwyn.

'I want to know,' said the goddess. 'Was he in love with his sister-in-law? Is that what you mean? I never heard that.'

Helena recalled the expression she had seen on his face when she had seen him in the secret room, looking at his sister-in-law's portrait.

'Why do you think she was running out to meet him that night — the night she died — when he came home from a neighbouring ball? She couldn't go to it with him, it would have made a scandal, but everyone knew they were in love with each other. She couldn't wait to see him and she went to him the moment he returned to the castle. They were lovers. Everyone knows it.'

'No!' said the goddess.

'Everyone knows no such thing,' retorted Nell Gwyn. 'It was a rumour, and nothing more. Some people have nothing better to do than to gossip about their neighbours.'

'He fell in love with her when his brother brought her to the castle just before their wedding,' went on Maid Marion, ignoring the interruption. 'She came with her family. It was her father who'd arranged the match. They stayed for a week and at the end of the week she was married. But when she said 'I do' to one brother, in her heart she was saying, 'I do' to the other.'

'Scandal and nonsense,' said Nell Gwyn, her oranges dancing with her emotion.

'I heard that she was besotted with him, but that he would not look at her,' piped up a buxom Viking. 'She set her cap at him, but he ignored her, so she married the other brother to spite him.'

'And I heard that he was madly in love with her, but that she was in love with her husband,' said an Italian contessa.

'Everyone — ' said the fairy, before stopping and looking at Helena.

All the women turned to look at her, finally realizing there was an outsider amongst them.

'Can you tell me where the ladies' withdrawing-room is?' asked Helena.

'I don't know, I'm sure,' said the goddess.

'The balls used to be so well arranged when his lordship's old housekeeper was here, but tonight I can find nothing I want. It is a pity she left in such a hurry. I wonder what became of her,' said Helena.

'Tempted away by higher wages,' said the Viking promptly. 'She went to Lady Abbinghale in London.'

'I heard it was the Honourable Mrs Ingle,' said Nell Gwyn, her interest caught.

'No, it was Lady Abbinghale. She steals everyone's servants. She stole Lord Camring's chef. Paid the man double, and left Lord Camring with no one to cook for him when he entertained the Prince. So then what does Lord Camring do but steal his chef back again at treble his original wages. We're slaves to our servants, and anyone who says otherwise doesn't know what they're talking about.'

'The withdrawing-room is at the end of the corridor, on the right,' said a young woman who had previously said nothing, and who was dressed as Lady Macbeth.

Helena was disappointed in the answer, for now she had no excuse to remain, but she thanked Lady Macbeth and moved away. She went into the withdrawing-room in case anyone was watching her, and adjusted her hat, settling it more firmly on her head. It was very tall, and it had a tendency to slip to one side. As she secured it with a pin, she noticed that the woman next to her was dressed as Katharine of Aragon, and she remembered

Mrs Willis saying that that would be her costume. More, she remembered Mrs Willis's strange manner when she had visited her, and found herself wondering about the rector's wife.

When Mrs Willis left the room, Helena followed her discreetly, and saw Mrs Willis going up the stairs as silently as a shadow. She reached the top, and caught a glimpse of Mrs Willis's hem going along the corridor until she reached a room at the end. She stopped and looked round furtively, and Helena shrank back against the wall. Appearing satisfied that no one was following her, Mrs Willis slipped into the room.

Helena followed, wondering what she would find. She reached the door and turned the handle slowly, hoping it would not creak. There was a slight noise as the door started to swing open and immediately she stopped, inching it open further when there was no commotion from within. She eventually opened it enough to see into the room, and what she saw shocked her. Mrs Willis was locked in a passionate embrace with a young Poseidon, a man who was clearly not her husband.

She hastily left the room, closing the door softly behind her. Mrs Willis was not all she seemed to be. If she was concealing a lover, could she possibly be concealing other things as well?

Helena's thoughts were whirling and she felt in need of some time to think. She was passing the long gallery and slipped inside. It was far away from the bustle of the ballroom, and she welcomed its coolness. The dim light was soothing. Here there were no candles and no mirrors, only the soft moonlight coming in through the windows. It was coloured by the stained glass, making red and blue patterns on the floor.

She began to pace the length of the gallery, walking in and out of the pools of coloured light as she thought over everything she had seen and heard. She had not gone more than halfway when she started, for there was a figure at the end. In the eerie light she could see no more than his silhouette, but she knew who he was at once, by a stirring of the air and a lift of something inside her. It was Lord Torkrow. She started to back away, but it was too late! He had heard her.

'We meet again,' he said, moving forward, his skin dappled red and then blue by the light. He looked down into her eyes. 'I wonder, was it by accident or design?'

'Forgive me, my lord, it was an accident,' she said. 'I did not know anyone was in here. I wanted to get away for a while. I did not mean to disturb you.'

'No matter,' he said. 'I was ready to rejoin my guests.'

'Then I must not prevent you,' she said, although she felt a powerful force emanating from him, and found it hard to turn away.

'I have changed my mind,' he said. 'It is time for the unmasking, and I am intrigued. Who are you?'

'I cannot tell you yet,' she prevaricated. 'It is still five minutes to midnight. I will unmask in the ballroom at the appointed hour.'

'Will you? Or will you disappear like a will-o'-the-wisp, never to be seen again?'

'Of course not,' she said. 'The idea is absurd.'

But, standing the in the long gallery, it did not seem absurd. The supernatural seemed to be all around them, from the dappled light to the strange atmosphere.

'I am not so sure,' he said. 'I am beginning to think you are a creature from folk tale who will evaporate as midnight strikes, leaving me bereft, and I have a mind to discover your identity now, before it is too late.'

'That would spoil the game entirely,' she said, turning to go.

He caught her by the arm and said, 'It is near enough the appointed time, and I will not be denied.'

So saying, he pulled off her mask. Its strings caught on her wig, and the mask, wig and hat came off together. She felt a surge of alarm and she had a desire to run away, but he was still holding her arm, and flight was impossible.

Her only hope lay in the dim light, but it was dashed as she saw recognition dawn in his eyes. For a long time, he just looked at her. And then he said again, 'Who are you?'

Helena's pulse jumped at the question. So he knew she wasn't Mrs Reynolds! Or perhaps he did not know for certain; perhaps he just had doubts; in which case, she must not confirm them.

'I know I should not have done it, but I could not resist. I heard the music and I was overcome with a longing to dance, and so I slipped upstairs and put on the costume I had been intending to wear for the servants' ball,' she said.

'Then if you want to dance, you must dance.'

He slipped his hand round her waist and before she knew what was happening, they were waltzing, whirling in and out of the shadows whilst the light played strange tricks all around them. Was he a man or a monster? she wondered, as the faint strains of music drifted up from the minstrels' gallery, like the wail of an unearthly creature howling in the dark.

'Well? Was it worth it?' he asked her, as they reached the end of the gallery.

'I cannot answer that,' she said, looking up at him and trying to read his thoughts.

'Why not?'

'Because I do not know yet what the consequences will be.'

'So, disguising yourself does not trouble you unless there are consequences?'

'That is not what I said.'

'But it is what you meant. Was it worth the deception, to get what you wanted? Did the end justify the means?'

She felt that he was not talking to her about her disguise, but about something much more sinister, and she began to be frightened. She tried to pull away from him, but he held her fast.

'Just what *would* you do, if you felt there would not be any consequences? You did not hesitate to impersonate Elizabeth Reynolds. What else would you not hesitate to do?'

'I don't understand you,' she said, feeling a rising tide of panic.

'Would you lie . . . steal . . . kill?'

His fingers tightened round her wrist like a vise.

'Let me go.'

With a strength born of desperation, she wrenched herself free, but he stood in front of her and would not let her pass.

'Who are you?' he demanded menacingly.

'I am Elizabeth Reynolds.'

'No, you are not Elizabeth Reynolds. She never arrived. A messenger arrived from York earlier this evening, saying that Mrs Reynolds had written to apologize for not taking up her position, because she had been ill, and was still not well enough to work. And so I ask you again, who are you? And what are you doing at Stormcrow Castle?'

For a brief moment she thought of telling him the truth, but it was too dangerous. If he had done away with her aunt, and if he knew she had come looking for her, then he would do away with her, too.

'A friend,' she said. 'I'm a friend of Mrs Reynolds. She told me she would not be able to take up the position as she was not well, but she did not want to acquire a reputation for being unreliable with the registry office. I was looking for a position at the time, and so we agreed that I would take her place.'

He looked at her searchingly, and then his face twisted.

'You are lying,' he said roughly. 'You will leave the castle first thing in the morning. The carriage will be at the door at seven o'clock. It will take you to the stagecoach. And to make sure you go, I will put you on the stage myself. You will leave this neighbourhood, and you will not return. If you do, I will know how to deal with you.'

His eyes were hard, and in the candlelight they glittered like obsidian. He loomed over her, and she wondered what he would be capable of if he was crossed. But she would never find out, because she had no intention of remaining. She had learnt all she could at the castle.

'Very well,' she said. She thought of the coming journey, and realized that she had no money. 'What of my wages?' she asked.

'Your wages?' he returned incredulously.

'I have worked for you faithfully, and my wages are owing,' she said defiantly.

He looked as though he was about to make a cutting retort, but then thought better of it.

'I will have them waiting for you in the morning,' he said. 'Make sure you are in the courtyard at five minutes to seven.'

'I will be there.'

And with that she picked up her mask, hat and wig, then swept past him, out of the gallery. Once she was out of sight she gave in to an urge to flee, and she ran back to her room, closing and locking the door behind her.

Only then did she let out a deep breath. She was safe at last. She went over to the fire and knelt in front of it, wrapping her arms around herself. As she did so, she began to shiver with reaction to the frightening encounter. She had not known what he would say or do, and at one point she had been afraid that she might not even escape with her life. Thoughts whirled round her head — graveyards and ballrooms, castles and crypts — all was jumble and confusion.

The fire was hot, with flames leaping in the grate, but it did little to warm her. She was cold through and through. She glanced at the bed, and wondered if there was a hot brick in it. She went over to it and discovered, to her relief, that there was. She undressed and slipped her nightdress over her head, then climbed between the sheets, but although she lay down and closed her eyes, Lord Torkrow aroused such conflicting emotions in her that she could not sleep.

At last she got out of bed and, throwing her shawl round her shoulders, she went over to the fire. Sitting beside it, she looked into the flames.

There was one chance more for her to learn something about her aunt. If she went to Mary and told her the truth, then perhaps Mary could tell her something.

The more she thought of it, the more the idea appealed to her. She would leave early, before the carriage was ready, for it would be better by far to be well away from the castle by the time he started looking for her. With Mary she would feel safe.

She went back to bed and at last she fell asleep, but vivid dreams gave her no rest. She was running through the castle, holding up the skirt of her medieval gown as she ran along the corridors, looking for something she could not find, her task made more difficult by a swirling mist. The mist parted, and she saw a door. She seemed to be moving in slow motion as she opened it, to reveal a large room with a four-poster bed, hung with red curtains. A man and woman were embracing passionately by the bed. As Helena watched, the woman opened her eyes and turned towards her, smiling as the man kissed her throat. And then the woman's face changed, becoming her own, and as the man spun round, Helena saw it was Lord Torkrow.

Shocked, she closed the door and ran on down the corridor, but it was hung with cobwebs. She brushed them aside, but they became thicker and thicker as she went along, until she was flailing wildly in an effort to keep them away from her. They were in her hair and her mouth, and they were beginning to suffocate her. She fought them wildly . . . and woke up to find that she was wrestling with the sheets. She was panting with the exertion, and she lay still, until she heard a noise and realized what had woken her: it was Effie, scratching on the door.

She rose, bleary eyed and feeling unrefreshed, and let the scullery maid into the room. As Effie saw to the fire, she washed and dressed. She put on her warmest clothes and her stout shoes, then she went down to the kitchen. It was empty apart from Effie, who had finished seeing to the fires and who was busy washing dishes.

'Where is Mrs Beal?' asked Helena.

'She's seeing to the clearing up,' said Effie.

Helena felt sorry to be leaving Mrs Beal to so much work. If things had been otherwise she would have overseen the servants as they returned the spare furniture to the attic and instructed them as they cleared the rooms, but she could not linger.

She helped herself to some rolls and chocolate, then sat by the fire to break her fast.

When she had done, she went upstairs and packed her few possessions. She checked the drawers and wardrobe to make sure that nothing had been forgotten, and looked under the bed, then closed her valise and set it by the door.

She glanced at the clock on the mantel-piece. It was nearly half past six.

Throwing her cloak over her shoulders, she put on her bonnet and pulled on her gloves then, picking up her valise went swiftly down the back stairs. She had hoped to see Mrs Beal before she left, but time was moving on and she did not want to risk looking for her in case she bumped into Lord Torkrow.

She opened the side door carefully and looked out. There was no one about. She went out, closing the door behind her.

She hurried across the courtyard, looking over her shoulder as she did so to make sure she was not being followed. She had a dread of seeing Lord Torkrow or Miss Parkins standing at one of the windows, watching her, and she scanned them nervously, but, to her relief, there was no one there.

Her gaze reached the gallery window . . . and her heart almost stopped, for she was suddenly reminded of the fact that the castle was symmetrical. Every room had its counterpart.

So the galleries must be symmetrical, and the hidden room in the portrait gallery must have its counterpart in the long gallery.

There was another secret room.

11

The enormity of the revelation froze her for a moment then, turning on her heel, she ran back to the castle. In the side door she went, up the stairs, along the corridor and into the long gallery. She walked along its length, her footsteps sounding loud to her ears, despite her attempts to walk quietly, and it was with relief that she reached the end of the gallery. She dropped her valise, and then began to feel the wainscoting, running both hands across it. There must be a way of opening it, and she guessed it must have something to do with the embossing. She pressed the flowers and turned the grapes and, as she did so, she called out softly, 'Aunt Hester! Aunt Hester! It's me, Helena!'

But there was no reply.

She pushed the centre of a small flower, and it gave. She heard a click, and then a door in the panelling swung open. She took a deep breath and went in.

She found herself in a small room. There was a window to the west, but the grey light of morning did little to illuminate the chamber. The air was stale, and she wrinkled her nose against it. She stood motionless whilst her eyes adjusted to the dim light and then went forward. As she did so, she saw that the room was empty, except for some blankets on the floor in the corner. There were no pictures on the walls, and the floor was bare.

She went over to the blankets, which had been arranged to make a bed. She crouched down next to them and turned them over, then she sat back, shocked, as she saw that, in between the folds was a piece of plaited lavender. She picked it up with trembling fingers. So her aunt had been here!

She shook the blankets, hoping to find another clue, and something fell out. It was a wooden soldier. She picked it up and examined it. It had been painted but the paint was coming off. It was evidently a much-loved and much-used child's toy. But what had a child been doing in this room, and what had Aunt Hester been doing with him?

Could the child have been playing here, and could Aunt Hester have been looking after him? But why would anyone make a child play in a cramped, gloomy apartment? And what child could it be? Lord Torkrow had never married.

But his brother had . . .

A sliver of fear crawled down her back. Every dark thing she had ever heard about Lord Torkrow and every unsettling thing she had experienced since entering the castle, returned to haunt her. Had he been responsible for her aunt's disappearance, and perhaps worse besides?

What had her aunt been doing in the secret room? Tending to the child? Or protecting him? Because if Lord Torkrow's brother had been the older of the two, and if he had had a son, then the boy was the true heir of Stormcrow Castle . . .

Helena left the room, closing the door behind her. There was a click, and then it merged into the wall.

She abandoned her plan to leave the neighbourhood, for she knew she could not ignore what she had found. She feared that a terrible crime had been perpetrated at the castle, but who to tell?

Her mind went back to the costume ball, and the man dressed as Harlequin: Sir Hugh Greer, the local Justice of the Peace.

Helena made up her mind to visit him and lay the facts before him: that her aunt had gone missing, and that she had found evidence of her aunt and a child having been kept in a secret room in the castle.

He would know what to do.

She did not know where to find him, so first she must go to Mary's cottage, for Mary would know, and she might even lend Helena the trap to take her there.

She picked up her valise and went down the stairs, moving cautiously. It was nearing seven o'clock. She could hear the sound of the carriage being brought round. The crunching of the gravel under the wheels was like the sound of bones, and a new fear assailed her. She had delayed so long that, if she set off on foot, she feared she would soon be caught because Lord Torkrow would overtake her in the carriage.

A quick glance out of the front door showed her that he had not yet appeared, and hurrying through the hall, she reached the carriage before he came in sight. Its black body seemed ominous, and she was afraid of climbing inside, to be swallowed by the red interior, but she mastered her dread as Eldridge climbed down from the box.

'His lordship has been delayed,' she said. 'You are to take me to Miss Debbet's cottage, where I am to deliver a message. You will then proceed to the stage post alone and await his lordship's instructions.'

'That's not what'e said to me,' said Eldridge, his dour face glowering suspiciously. ''E said I was to go to the stage, but'e didn't say nothing about no cottage.'

'He has changed his mind. If you don't believe me, then you must go and ask him yourself. He is in his study. But make haste! He has commanded me to deliver his message without delay.'

She climbed into the carriage. Eldridge looked towards the door, then at Helena's impassive face, and gave a brief nod before folding the step and shutting her in. He mounted his box, and then they were away. She breathed a sigh of relief to think that one problem, at least, had been overcome.

The carriage seemed to crawl away from the castle, and she sat forward on her seat, willing it to go faster. At any minute she expected Lord Torkrow to emerge from the castle, shouting, 'Stop!'

She was so fearful that she could not help looking back, but everything was quiet. The carriage rolled on slowly, through the arch, and then it began to pick up speed as it emerged on to the road.

She looked forward again, but her eyes did not see the moor as it rolled past. Instead they turned inwards, and she was consumed by her thoughts. What had really happened at the castle? Had Lord Torkrow tried to murder his nephew, and had Aunt Hester hidden the boy in an effort to protect him? If so, where had she gone? Had she taken the child with her? And was she alive, or were they both . . . ? She did not want to finish the thought.

The carriage turned off the main road and she recalled her thoughts from their dark paths. Ahead of her, she could see Mary's cottage. Never had a sight been more welcome. She opened the door as the carriage rolled to a halt and jumped out. Eldridge looked surprised at her behaviour, but said nothing, merely closing the door behind her.

'Go on to the stage post and await his lordship's further instructions,' she said.

At least, if Sir Hugh had to force his way into the castle, he would find one less man blocking his way.

Eldridge looked dubious, but he nodded his head, and the carriage rolled away. As soon as he had gone, Helena went up the path and knocked at the door. It was early, but she hoped Mary would be awake.

She need not have worried. The door was opened by the maid, and she was shown in, to find Mary sitting in the parlour.

'Mrs Reynolds,' said Mary, standing up in surprise.

'I am sorry to disturb you at such an hour, but I am in dire need of help,' said Helena without preamble, afraid that at any moment there could be a knock on the door and that Lord Torkrow could walk in.

'Whatever has happened?' asked Mary in concern. 'Has there been an accident? Is someone hurt? Are you ill?'

'Please, have the trap readied. I will explain everything when it is brought round.'

Mary looked surprised, but she hesitated for only a moment, and then she gave the maid instructions to see that the trap was to be brought round to the front door.

'And tell Tom to make haste,' she said, as the maid left the room.

'Thank you,' said Helena gratefully.

'I do not know where you need to go in such a hurry, but won't you have something to eat whilst we wait?' said Mary. 'I was just having breakfast, and you cannot set off until the horse has been harnessed. Some food will help sustain you on the journey ahead, wherever you are going.'

Helena accepted gratefully. She had already breakfasted, but it seemed a long time ago. Mary poured her a cup of chocolate and handed it to her with a piece of seed cake. Helena ate gratefully, then accepted a second cup of chocolate, but she left it half finished as she heard the trap outside. She leapt up.

'I must go at once.'

Mary rose calmly and followed her into the

hall, putting on her cloak.

'I do not know what has happened, but I think you need a friend,' said Mary. 'I cannot let you go off by yourself. I am coming with you.'

Helena felt a rush of relief. With the groom and Mary beside her, she would feel much safer if Lord Torkrow should happen to ride after the carriage and come across her on the way.

'I would be glad of your company,' said Helena.

'Then come, let us be off.'

Together they went outside.

'Now, where to?' asked Mary, as she followed Helena into the trap.

'Sir Hugh Greer's house,' said Helena. 'I need to see a justice of the peace.'

'But isn't Lord Torkrow the nearest justice?' asked Mary with a frown.

'Yes, he is, but I cannot speak to him. It is about him I have to lay a complaint.'

Mary looked surprised, and she seemed about to protest, but then she simply instructed the groom to drive to Sir Hugh's house.

'Now, don't you think you had better tell me what this is all about?' she asked, once they were safely on their way.

Helena gave a deep sigh.

'There is so much I have to tell you.' She could maintain the deception no longer, and she was relieved to be able to tell Mary the truth. 'First of all, you must know that I am not Mrs Reynolds,' she said, and then her story came pouring out in a rush.

Mary listened silently, and when the recital was over, she said, 'So you think Lord Torkrow has hidden his brother's son, or done something worse, so that he can rob the boy of his inheritance, and keep the title and the castle for himself?'

'I am afraid it is possible, yes,' she said.

'It seems incredible,' said Mary musingly. 'And yet you found a hidden room, with your aunt's plaited lavender and the child's toy, and your aunt is definitely missing.'

'Yes,' Helena agreed. 'You were concerned as well, weren't you?' she asked. 'You were worried about my aunt? Your story about needing to return a book to her was a ruse, so that you could find out her forwarding address?'

Mary nodded. 'It was. I thought, if you had an address for her, then I could find her. How did you guess?'

'I knew the book could not belong to my aunt. She had never had much time for reading, and as far as I know she has never owned a book. Besides, she does not like poetry.'

'Ah. I see. It was a poor story, but it was the best I could think of at the time. You do not blame me for the ruse?'

'Not at all. I am grateful to you for it, and for trying to find her. I hope she is all right, but with every passing day and still no word . . . ' said Helena anxiously.

'Perhaps word has reached your lodgings?'

'No, my friend collects the mail and would have sent me news.'

'Even so, things might not be as bad as you fear. Perhaps your aunt managed to escape with the child. If she needed to retreat to a place of safety, where would she go?'

'I cannot think of anywhere,' said Helena, as she turned her mind to this new possibility.

'Does she have any relatives she could turn to?'

'No, only me, and she did not come to me.'

'But she must have taken him somewhere,' said Mary thoughtfully. 'Can you not think of anywhere?'

'No. Unless . . . Mrs Beal mentioned that the old butler, Vance, went to live in Hull, when he and his wife retired. My aunt had worked with Vance before, and it was he who had recommended her for the position at the castle — '

'Then that's where she must have gone. Never fear, you will find her yet. Do you know exactly whereabouts in Hull the butler lives?'

'No. I never thought to ask.'

'Why should you? But it is of no importance. We will go there and seek them out. They cannot be hard to find. Someone will know of them by name, or of a woman and a child who are newly arrived in the town. You do not object to my plan? If you wish, we can continue on our way and consult Sir Hugh, but it is not certain that he will be at home, or that he will believe us. And even if he does, he might not like to move against a neighbour, particularly not one of Lord Torkrow's standing. It seems to me that we would be better finding your aunt and the boy ourselves.'

Helena agreed. For the first time in many weeks she had hope. If only Mary was right, then she might be seeing Aunt Hester before the day was out.

They had travelled some miles across the moor, and were approaching The Dog and Cart. Mary suggested they should change the horse before going on.

'We will ask for a hamper to take with us, too. We might be delayed on the journey, and it could take us hours to find the right address. It will be quicker if we eat on the road, rather than wasting time looking for an inn once we reach Hull.'

Helena agreed, and when they pulled up in the yard, Mary suggested that Helena go inside to order the food, whilst she made sure the horse was changed for a satisfactory animal.

Helena climbed down and went into the inn. It was a small but respectable establishment, and as she entered, the innkeeper came forward to greet her. She told him what she wanted, and he showed her into a private parlour until the provisions should be ready.

The parlour had a table and two settles, but Helena was too restless to sit down. She paced the room, anxious to be on her way again.

The innkeeper seemed to be taking a long time with the provisions. She went out into the corridor to find him, but as she did so, she was horrified to see Lord Torkrow walking in at the inn's main door at the far end of the corridor.

She shrank back, wondering what he was doing there. Had he followed her, or was his presence there a coincidence? Perhaps he had decided to ride to the stage post when he had discovered the carriage was missing, and perhaps he had stopped at the inn to find if the carriage had passed. Once he had learnt what he wanted to know, she hoped he would be on his way again, but until then she would have to stay out of sight.

She ran back along the corridor and slipped back into the parlour. She listened intently, every nerve straining, but she heard nothing and began to relax. And then she heard footsteps coming down the corridor. They made an ominous clicking noise as they crossed the flagged floor, and stopped outside the door. But was it the innkeeper, or was it Lord Torkrow?

She saw the door knob turning, and, suddenly panicking, she leant against the door, but it heaved, and in a moment it was flung open. She was thrown back against the wall, but by good fortune she was hidden by the door. She saw Lord Torkrow stride into the room like a dark creature of the night, intent on finding his prey. Helena shrank back.

He looked round, and for a moment she thought he would not see her, but then his eyes alighted on her and he closed the door, revealing her.

'So,' he said menacingly. 'This is where you are. Then it is as I had suspected. You took a post in the castle under false pretences. Well, your master will be disappointed. You will not be able to tell him anything.'

'My master?' she asked in confusion,

wondering what he was talking about.

'Or did you not see him? Has he remained in the shadows? Is it only Maria you have dealt with? Then you are fortunate. And I suppose it is possible, for she could pay you as well as he.'

Helena was perplexed.

'I don't know what you're talking about,' she said.

'No?'

He took her arm and pulled her over to the window. She saw the trap, complete with a fresh horse. Mary's coachman was climbing up on to the box, and Mary herself was already in the trap. They were ready to leave. She must go to them!

Pulling free of him, she ran for the door and wrenched it open. But then a sound from the yard gave her pause, a clattering on the cobbles, and turning her head she saw that the trap had set off without her. She ran to the window and in a lightning quick move, threw it open, and shouted, 'Mary!'

Mary turned her head and saw her, but then she turned away and the trap continued across the yard.

Helena was dumbfounded. Why had Mary deserted her? Had Lord Torkrow paid her to leave? Impossible! Mary would not give in to intimidation or bribery, she was sure. But the trap continued, and turned into the road.

Lord Torkrow joined her at the window and said savagely, 'Damn you! So she was here after all. And where she is, he will not be far behind. Where is she going? What have you told her? You found the secret room, but what more have you learnt? Answer me! What have you told her? Where is she going?'

Helena did not know why Mary had left her, but she knew one thing: she could not answer his question if she wanted her aunt to be safe.

'I will tell you nothing,' she said, rounding on him.

'You will tell me everything I want to know, or it will be the worse for you,' he said threateningly.

'Never,' she said, between gritted teeth.

'I don't know what you think to gain by protecting them. They have already paid you — or perhaps not,' he added appraisingly. 'Perhaps that is why you are protecting them. Perhaps you are afraid they will go back on their part of the bargain if you give them away.'

'I don't know what you're talking about,' she said.

'Tell me, *have* they paid you?' he asked roughly.

'Have who paid me?'

'Maria and Morton'

'I don't know anyone by the name of Maria, but if you mean Mary, why should she pay me? I do not work for her.'

'Then you work for Morton.'

'I know no one by the name of Morton. The only man I have ever seen her with is her brother, and surely even you would not blacken the character of a poor, sick man who was wounded at the Battle of Waterloo in defence of his country?' she returned scathingly.

He regarded her closely, then said: 'You are a very good actress, or they have lied to you.'

'They have never told me anything, other than that they were living in the country for the good of Mr Debbet's health. You are either evil or mad.'

He searched her face.

'And you are either a hapless pawn or a willing accomplice, but it makes no difference,' he said. 'Where were you going with Maria?'

'I don't know,' she said.

'You do, and you will tell me,' he said brutally.

'Do you really believe I would deliver a woman and a child up to you, so that you can finish what you have begun? Do your worst. You will never have them,' she flared.

He looked at her curiously, then asked her the question he had asked her in the gallery. 'Who are you?' he said.

'Your nemesis,' she returned.

'Your name,' he demanded.

She flung it at him defiantly, glad to be rid of the pretence. 'My name is Carlisle,' she said. 'I am Mrs Carlisle's niece.'

He look shocked, then said, as if to himself, 'So that is it. The handkerchief — C. Carlisle.'

She saw understanding dawn on his face, and she wondered what he was going to do, now that he knew the truth. Would he imprison her as he had imprisoned her aunt?

Her question was soon answered, for saying 'There's no time to waste', he took her hand and pulled her along in his wake as he strode out of the parlour. 'You are coming with me,' he said.

She resisted, but he was too strong for her. She looked about her for help, but the corridor was empty. He pulled her towards the entrance, through which she could see his carriage. So! He had caught up with it, and learned of her ruse.

She dug her heels into the gap between the flags, knowing that if she climbed into the carriage she would be at his mercy. It gave her the resistance she needed to bring him to a halt.

'There is no escape,' he said, tightening his grip. 'You are coming with me, and you will tell me everything I need to know on the way.'

'So that you can find my aunt, and kill your nephew, as you killed your brother?' she demanded.

'*What?*' he said, rounding on her.

In his surprise he dropped her arm, and she ran, but she had only gone a few feet when he caught her again.

'You will never find them,' she said, turning on him. 'My aunt has hidden the boy, and she will look after him until Mary rescues them.'

He suddenly dropped her arm, and to her shock, his hand cupped her face. He looked deeply into her eyes.

'I don't know what Maria has told you,' he said, 'but I am not your enemy.'

Again, his words confused her.

'Who is Maria, and why do you keep talking about her?' she asked.

'She is the woman you arrived with at the inn. She is dangerous. I don't know how she has imposed on you, but I must know where she is going, because if she finds your aunt before we do, then she is likely to kill her.'

He was so convincing that she faltered.

'I don't know what to believe,' she said uncertainly.

Lord Torkrow was the villain, wasn't he?

But somehow his words had the ring of truth, and he was no longer behaving like a villain. He was not threatening her. He had dropped her hand and although he could have dragged her to the carriage and thrown her in, he had not done so.

'Your aunt is in danger, and so is my nephew,' he said. 'You have to decide who to trust; I cannot take the decision for you. You must trust Maria, or you must trust me.'

She felt very still. She remembered everything she had heard about him, every whisper, every rumour, and then she thought of her own experiences at the castle. He had been hostile, but she had never seen him do anything amiss: he had never mistreated the servants, and he had not filled the castle with debauched friends. Even his hostility could be explained if Mary was dangerous, as he claimed, and if he had thought she was in league with Mary.

But Mary could not be dangerous . . . could she? Helena thought of everything she knew about Mary, and was surprised to realize it was so little, and that even that little came from Mary herself. She remembered that Mary had tried to discover her aunt's whereabouts by pretending she had a poetry book belonging to her and asking for a forwarding address; and then again by saying that her aunt must have run away with the boy, and asking if Helena knew where they might have gone. And Mary had abandoned her at the inn as soon as she had learnt what she wanted to know.

Helena looked at the man in front of her, and thought of everything that had passed between them since she had entered the castle. He was dark and dangerous and she was half afraid of him, but she realized that her fear had never been for her safety. She was not, nor had she ever been, afraid he would hurt her, no matter how he had behaved; she was afraid because he awakened feelings in her that she could neither control nor ignore.

'Well?' he said. 'What is it to be? Do you trust Maria, or do you trust me?'

'I trust you,' she said.

He gave a ghost of a smile, then said: 'We must go.'

'My aunt is in — '

'Hull. I know. All I need to know now is if that is where Maria has gone.'

'Yes, it is.'

They went out into the corridor. The landlord was bustling towards them with a hamper. Lord Torkrow paid him a guinea, and gave him another, saying, 'Tell me, which is the best way to Hull?'

'Why, bless me, you're the second person to ask me that this morning. The young lady was just making enquiries. You follow the road here until you reach the main road . . . '

Helena grew more and more impatient as the man went on. She could not understand why Lord Torkrow listened patiently to the innkeeper's directions. Surely he knew the way?

'Thank you,' said Lord Torkrow.

The landlord went about his business, and they went out into the courtyard.

'Why did you ask for directions?' she said.

'Because I hoped that Maria might have done the same, and then I could discover which way the landlord had sent her. He will have told her the main route, as he told me, but it is not the quickest. We will beat her yet.'

His carriage was waiting for them. Fresh horses had been harnessed, and were champing at the bit. Eldridge opened the door and let down the step. Lord Torkrow stood back, letting Helena go in, and then followed her inside. The step was folded, the door closed, and as soon as Eldridge had climbed on to his box they were on their way.

Helena remembered the last time she had been in a carriage with him. How long ago it seemed! She had been afraid of him, and worried about her aunt. She was still worried.

Where had Aunt Hester gone? And why?

'Why did my aunt leave the castle?' she said. 'Did you send her away with your brother's child? And why?'

'Yes, I sent her away, but she was glad to go. She wanted to protect George as much as I did, and she knew it was the best way.'

'But why was he in danger? His parents are dead, so surely you are the boy's guardian?'

'My nephew is not the son of my brother. My brother died childless. The boy is my sister's son.'

'Your sister?'

'Yes. My sister. Anna. You saw her portrait.'

Helena cast her mind back to the portrait gallery and remembered the family portrait hanging there. It had shown Lord Torkrow and his brother as children, and there had been a little girl standing next to them.

'She was a beautiful girl,' he said with a far-away look on his face. 'She had soft, dark hair and a mouth that was made to smile. She was my father's favourite child, and my brother and I did not mind, because she was a favourite with us as well. She was the youngest, and we all took pleasure in looking after her.'

He turned to her. 'I owe you an explanation. I did not know you were Mrs Carlisle's niece, and so I said nothing about your aunt when you came to the castle. But you must be worried.'

'Yes, I am.'

'She is safe, in Hull, with my sister. My sister has not had a happy life,' he explained. 'When she was eighteen years old, my parents took her to London for a Season. She met a man there, John Morton, and she quickly became besotted with him. My father was displeased. Morton was older than her by some fifteen years. My father's warnings fell on deaf ears, however, because Morton had a way with women, and my sister was entranced.

'My father hoped it would come to nothing, that Morton would tire of her and turn to someone nearer his own age, but instead, Morton asked for her hand in marriage. My father was reluctant to agree, but Anna was in love, and so he gave his consent.

'At first all went well. Anna was happy, living with her husband in Norfolk. But then things started to change. She seemed quiet and withdrawn. I was anxious, and one day I paid her a surprise visit. I found her with a bruised face, and I told her she must leave her husband and come back with me to the castle, where my father, my brother — for he was still alive at the time — and I would protect her. She refused. I thought of carrying her bodily out of the manor house, but she told me she was with child. Her husband had been delighted with the news, she said. He had stopped hitting her, and had told her that he had only done it because he had been frustrated at the lack of an heir.

'I called on Anna many times over the next few years. My brother and sister-in-law also called on her, often unexpectedly, to make sure she was all right. She never had any bruises, and she was radiantly happy. She loved her little boy, and her husband doted on the child, too.

'I was reassured. Besides, I had other things to think of. My sister-in-law and my brother both died. Anna came to the funeral, but she never visited the castle after that, and I never went to the manor. I was lost in my own labyrinth of darkness, and had no thought to spare for anyone else.

'So things went on. And then came a day, a few months ago, when, on a wild night, my sister came to the castle. She was almost collapsing with exhaustion when I took her in, and she had been badly beaten. The mark of a whip was on her back — but I will say no more. Her cur of a husband had taken to hitting her again, and she had borne it silently, because she had known that if she left him he would never let her see her son again. But then he had threatened little George. She waited until he became unconscious through drink and, persuading a groom to help her, she took her son and set out for the castle.

'She had a little money, which she had kept hidden from her husband, and she used it on a ticket for the stagecoach, before walking the last part of the journey.

'Even when she reached the castle she did not feel safe. She was terrified that her husband might follow her, and so I took her to the attic, and I called on Mrs Carlisle to take care of her and the boy.'

'So that is why the maid heard crying in the attic,' said Helena. 'It was George.'

'Yes. The rumours spread. It was easy to dismiss the sound as ghosts amongst the villagers, but I knew that if Morton came near, he would know well enough what it meant. I moved Anna and the boy to the secret room, but even so, Anna did not want to stay at the castle — she lived in hourly dread of him finding her — but she was by this time too ill to leave. She had caught a fever, travelling through the cold and the snow. And so I asked your aunt if she would take little George to Hull, where Mr and Mrs Vance would care for him. She agreed readily. She felt sorry for my sister and nephew. She was to stay with George until my sister was well enough to join her in Hull, and then my sister would go to Italy, where she has a godmother. Anna would be able to raise her son in safety, somewhere her husband would never find her.'

'But I still don't understand about Mary — Maria,' said Helena.

'She is Morton's mistress, and would do anything for him. I followed you this morning — I left the castle in time to see the carriage disappearing into the distance, so I saddled a horse and rode after it. I lost it for a time, and rode aimlessly across the moor, but then I caught sight of it heading towards the stage post. When I arrived there, Eldridge told me he had taken you to Mary's cottage. I rode across the moor and saw you setting out in the trap, and I was finally able to catch up with you at the inn. I saw Maria clearly as I relinquished my horse to one of the ostlers, and I recognized her at once. I assumed you must be in league with her.'

'And so you followed me into the inn.'

'Yes. I wanted to know who you were and what you had told her. I also wanted to know where Morton was. I knew he would not be far from Maria.'

'I have met him, I think,' said Helena. 'He is tall, with dark hair and a slack face?'

'Yes. That is the result of the drink. But how did you meet him?'

'He and Mary — Maria — took a cottage near the castle. I met Maria when I was out walking one day. It came on to rain and she invited me in to shelter.'

'That was a fortunate meeting for her. Otherwise, if she had not come across you accidentally, she would have had to approach you at church.'

'She introduced me to Morton, but she said he was her brother. She tried to find out where my aunt had gone by saying Aunt Hester had left a book in the cottage. She asked for a forwarding address.'

'Ah, that was clever.'

'I knew the talk of the book was a ruse, but at the time I thought — '

'Yes?'

'I thought that you had done away with my aunt, and I thought Mary was worried about my aunt's disappearance, too.'

'And now? Are you convinced I have not done your aunt any harm?'

'Yes, I believe I am.'

He smiled. She had never seen such a smile on his face. It was like a sliver of sunshine on a squally day.

'May I know your name? Your true name?' he asked.

'It is Helena.'

'I am pleased to meet you, Helena Carlisle,' he said. 'Even though you have caused me a great deal of unease over the last few weeks,' he added with a wry smile.

'Did you suspect I was an impostor from the beginning?' she asked curiously.

'No, not then. I thought there was something you were hiding, but when I saw you had no wedding ring I thought you were lying about being married. You seemed very young, and I thought you had lied about your age in order to secure a position.'

'I was dismayed when you looked at my finger,' she said. 'I began to realize it would be difficult to keep up the pretence. When did you begin to suspect I might be in league with your brother-in-law?'

'It is difficult to know. From the beginning, I felt that something was not right, but I did not know what. You were more outspoken than my previous housekeepers, and you asked more questions. Then, too, you seemed very interested in the attic. It could just have been a natural desire to explore the castle, or indeed it could have been fear: you could have heard the rumours about ghosts and wanted to set your mind at rest. But when Miss Parkins found the handkerchiefs in your room embroidered with the initials C we began to be more suspicious, although we still could not be certain. Neither of us realized the truth, that the C stood for Carlisle. We both thought it stood for a Christian name: Catherine, Caroline . . . we thought of every name, and tried to remember if Morton had known any women whose names had begun with C. We could not recall one, but he had many women and we did not know them all.'

'I was alarmed when I knew Miss Parkins had been in my room, and it was worse when I realized she had found the handkerchiefs,' said Helena. 'She made me feel like a mouse being watched by a cat. I was frightened of her.'

'And you were wise to be so. She is a formidable adversary. She came to the castle with my mother, when my mother was a bride, and she was devoted to her, as she was devoted to my mother's children. If you had meant harm to my sister, Miss Parkins would have stopped at nothing to protect her.'

The carriage turned to the right and ahead of them there was softer countryside. They were leaving the moors behind. In the distance, a town could be seen. Smoke was rising from the chimneys. To the people who lived there, it was an ordinary day. They were paying visits, shopping, visiting the circulating library, going riding, attending to business

. . . but to Helena, it was a day of hope and revelation.

'Why did you not turn me out of the castle?' she asked, as the carriage finally turned into the main road and bowled along between houses and neatly kept gardens.

'Because if you were innocent, I did not want to deprive you of your livelihood, and if you were a pawn of Morton's I wanted you close by, so that I could watch you. And so I bided my time.'

'Until I showed my hand by taking your carriage?'

'Yes.'

'And so now what do we do?'

'We go to Hull. We hope to arrive before Maria and Morton. We tell Anna she can delay no longer, and we put her and her son on a ship bound for Italy.'

12

They fell into a companionable silence. Now that she was no longer afraid of him, Helena felt herself relax in his company. There was a softer side to him, one she had only glimpsed, but one she would like to know better.

But that was unlikely, she told herself. She would have no reason to remain at the castle once she had found her aunt. She would have to leave, and, unless she visited her aunt in the future, she would never see him again. She felt her spirits sink. He had become important to her, and she could not bear to think of their parting. She looked out of the window in an attempt to distract her thoughts.

They were now travelling along busier roads, which were better kept than those on the moors. There were fewer ruts, and the potholes were not so frequent. Helena watched the scenery change, going from countryside to town, and finally to coast. As the coach crested a hill, she saw the sea sparkling blue and placid beneath her. There was the cry of sea gulls, and the smell of salt was in the air. She licked her lips, and found that she could taste it.

'We are almost there,' he said.

Helena felt her interest quicken. She would soon see Aunt Hester again! And she would see Lord Torkrow's sister. She wondered what Anna would be like. She tried to remember the portrait, but she could remember very little, and besides, Anna had been much younger there. She was dark, that much Helena remembered, but little more.

The carriage rolled to a halt outside a small cottage. The coachman opened the door and let down the step. Helena climbed out. She was immediately hit by the wind, which tried to whip the bonnet from her head, and she held on to it, to prevent it blowing away. Her cloak was whipped around her ankles, and the sound of the wind battered her ears.

'It is often blustery on the coast,' he said, following her.

They went up to the door. As he lifted the knocker he looked all round, and Helena, too, was vigilant, knowing that, at any moment, Maria and Morton could appear.

The curtain moved a little and Helena caught sight of a face at the window. It was an elderly woman with an anxious look. As soon as the woman saw Lord Torkrow, however, her look of anxiety faded and was replaced with a smile. A minute later the door opened.

'My lord,' she said. 'We did not expect to see you.' Then her smile faded. 'Is something wrong?'

'I think we had better talk inside,' he said.

He stood back so that Helena could precede him. The woman gave her a curious look, but no more, and Helena found herself in a cosy hall. There was a staircase rising to her left, and ahead of her was a door leading to the back of the house. Beyond the staircase was another door, and it was through this that Helena was shown. She found herself in a whitewashed room, which was furnished with a blue sofa, blue curtains and a blue rug. Standing by the sofa, her knitting abandoned, was Aunt Hester.

'Aunt Hester!' said Helena, going forward and taking her hands.

'My dear Helena!' cried her aunt in astonishment. 'What are you doing here?'

'I wanted to see you, and I arrived at the castle to find you had gone.'

'My poor Helena. You went all that way for nothing. It was good of Lord Torkrow to bring you here,' she said. She looked searchingly at Helena. 'I can see from your face there is a lot you have to tell me, but now is not the time. I fear you bring bad news with you?'

'We do,' said Lord Torkrow. 'Morton is on

his way here. Where is Anna?'

Aunt Hester glanced at a door behind her, and Lord Torkrow went through. Helena followed him into a small room at the back of the house. It was brightly furnished, and there was a cheery fire in the grate. A woman and a little boy were playing on the rug in front of the fire, where the boy was lining up a row of toy soldiers. The woman looked up.

'Simon!' she exclaimed, jumping up in delight and embracing him. 'I am so glad to see you.'

As Helena witnessed the warmth between brother and sister, she thought that she had never known he could be so affectionate, and that to be loved by such a man would be something indeed.

Anna's face became anxious. 'My husband has found me?'

'Yes, my dear, he has.'

'I knew it would happen,' said Anna. 'I am only grateful it took him so long. At least I have had time to regain my health.'

She looked at Helena.

Quickly, Lord Torkrow introduced Helena and explained her presence, then said, 'There is no time to lose.'

Anna nodded, her expression grave.

'We must go. Once we are out of the country we will be safe from him. I have a bag packed already. I have had it packed ever since I arrived. Come, George, it is time for us to go on our journey.'

'To stay with Godmama?' asked the little boy.

'Yes, to stay with Godmama in Italy.'

'I'm going on a ship,' the boy said to Helena. 'A big ship. It's going to take me over the sea to a hot country where there are lots of flowers and we're going to live by the sea. We can go out, not like here. Here we have to stay indoors.'

A shadow crossed his face.

'But when we are in Italy, we will not have to hide any more,' Anna told him.

She took him out of the room to put on his outdoor clothes.

'You know what you do when he gets here?' said Lord Torkrow to the Vances.

'Yes, my lord, that we do. We'll send him to the cemetery so that he can see the grave.'

Helena looked at Lord Torkrow questioningly.

'I knew he would never let Anna go, so I had my stonemason make a headstone for her and my nephew,' he said. 'One night, we placed it in an out of the way corner in the graveyard. When her husband arrives, the Vances will tell him that she came here with the boy, but that she died soon afterwards and the boy followed her to the grave.'

'Will he believe it?'

'I think so. He beat them both badly, and it was snowing when they escaped. It is not unlikely that they would have caught a fever on their flight and, already weakened by the beating, have succumbed. It is, at all events, worth a try.'

Anna and George returned, ready for their journey. George was prattling happily about Italy as they all went out to the carriage.

Helena saw that Aunt Hester was dressed for a journey.

'I am going with Anna, as her chaperon,' she said, 'but once I've seen her safely to her godmother's house, I'll return. Will you wait for me at the castle? Then I can tell you everything.'

'Of course,' said Helena.

She sat next to her aunt in the carriage. Anna sat opposite them, with Simon next to her, and little George on her knee.

'There's a ship sailing to Italy this evening,' said Anna. 'I've taken notice of their comings and goings, and I always know when the next ship will sail. I would have left soon anyway. I have regained my health, and I was only waiting to regain my strength completely before leaving.'

'But you are strong enough for the

journey?' asked Simon in concern.

'Yes. I have Mrs Carlisle with me. We will manage.'

The cry of the gulls became louder as they approached the sea. The wind stiffened and the carriage swayed from side to side. The streets became busier. Carts were heading for the dock, laden with sacks and barrels. Women in rough skirts and thick woollen shawls jostled seamen, who swore and cursed and spat. There was a smell of fish, overlaid with the pervading smell of salt, and there was a clamour of creaking rigging which mixed in with the clatter of wheels on cobblestones and the sound of sailors' cries.

As they neared the water, their progress became much slower as Eldridge picked his way between carts and carriages, avoiding urchins and stray dogs, until he finally stopped by the shipping office.

The door opened and the step was let down. Simon climbed out first, looking round with alertness in case Maria had caught up with them. Anna followed, with George, then Helena stepped out with Aunt Hester.

A cry of 'Anna!' rent the air, and Helena looked round in horror, but it was not Maria. It was an elderly woman, who was waving to a young girl, another, different, Anna.

Helena breathed a sigh of relief, and they

went into the office.

The arrangements were soon made. Anna's ship was to sail with the evening tide. As they emerged once more on to the dock, they saw the ship not far off. Looking around all the time, they crossed the dock and reached the vessel.

As she set foot on the gangplank, Helena felt it sway in the breeze and she clutched the rope, provoking laughter from a sailor nearby. Regaining her dignity, she ran up the remainder of the gangplank and was relieved to be on the ship.

Interested in all she heard and saw, she accompanied the small party to Anna's cabin. It was surprisingly well appointed, and George ran round it in delight.

'Will you stay with me until I sail?' Anna asked Simon.

'Yes. There are some things I must see to, first, but I will not leave the ship.'

She glanced at Helena, then nodded and gave her attention to her son.

'Will you join me?' said Simon to Helena.

'Of course,' she said.

They did not go on deck; they would be too obvious should Maria arrive; but they stood outside the cabin, talking.

'I want you to return to the castle,' he said.

'But would it not be easier for me to stay

with you? The ship sails in a few hours, and we could return together.'

'I do not want you here. If Morton finds us, things could get ugly. It is bad enough that I cannot protect Anna from such a scene, if he arrives. I will not have you exposed to it. Take the carriage. Return to the castle. I will hire an equipage once the ship sets sail and join you later. And then we will have much to discuss.'

Her dismissal, and her wages, she thought, with a sinking feeling. Her time at the castle was drawing to its end.

'Very good, my lord.'

Helena returned to the cabin to take her leave. She embraced Aunt Hester, wished Anna a safe journey, and then she left the ship. As she set foot on the gangplank she looked around the dock, but there was still no sign of Maria. Bracing herself for the swaying underfoot, she succeeded in reaching the dock without difficulty, and then she went over to the carriage.

'We are to return to the castle,' she said. 'His lordship will follow.'

Eldridge nodded, then Helena climbed into the carriage and it pulled away, the horses' hoofs clattering on the cobblestones as they left the harbour.

Simon watched the carriage as it pulled

away, and found himself wishing he was going with it. He wanted to see Anna safely on her way, but he wanted to be with Helena, too. He could finally acknowledge his feelings, now that he knew who she was, and he found they were even deeper than he had suspected. But to acknowledge them and to welcome them were two different things.

He returned to the cabin. Mrs Carlisle was playing with George, and Anna was watching them. She turned her head as he entered and said: 'Has she gone?'

'Yes. I have sent her back to the castle.'

'I feel in need of a breath of air,' said Anna.

'You cannot go on deck, it is not safe.'

'In the corridor, then. You will come with me?'

He agreed, and together they went into the corridor.

'You like her,' she said, when they were alone.

'Yes. I do,' he said.

He had never been able to keep anything from Anna, even when they had been children, for she had always known what he was thinking, and it was a relief to say the words out loud.

'I am glad,' she said with a sigh. 'You have suffered too much, Simon. I think you should marry her, and be happy at last.'

He shook his head.

'Love does not bring happiness,' he said, his mood darkening.

'It brought happiness to Richard.'

'It brought him torture!' he returned.

'I don't understand you,' she said, puzzled.

'You did not see him as I did, Anna. It was I who had to carry him the news; it was I who had to tell him I'd killed his wife. It was I who destroyed his world.'

She touched his hand.

'It was an accident, Simon. You cannot blame yourself.'

'Can I not? If I had not returned to the castle when I did, she would still be alive.'

'You could not know she would run out to greet you.'

'For a moment . . . one moment . . . I thought she wanted to see me,' he said, as he remembered his elation at seeing her, and seeing the smile on her lips. 'But she thought it was Richard, returning from the Doyles. It was dark, the horse was startled . . . '

'You could not help it,' she said gently. 'No blame attached to you.'

'I remember it all so clearly. It is etched on my memory. I can still see her running up to my horse and being knocked aside. I can see her falling, I can remember how I felt as I leapt from the saddle and tried to catch her, but it all happened so quickly, and before I knew what was happening she was lying on the ground with a trickle of blood wetting her hair. If there had not been a stone just there, where she had fallen, she might still be alive, but it was jagged and she hit her head . . . I can still remember my anguish when I knew she was dead.'

'You loved her,' said Anna quietly.

'No,' he said. 'I simply thought I did. I picked her up and carried her inside, fancying my feelings the grief of love, but when I told Richard . . . when he understood she was dead . . . I saw the pit of hell open up in his eyes. I had never, until that moment, known what love was, but I knew it then, and it terrified me. My feelings had been but a pale reflection. I decided at that moment that I would never fall in love. I never wanted to open myself up to such pain.'

'We cannot choose where or when we will love,' she said softly.

'I choose, and I have chosen.'

'Then I pity you,' she said sadly, 'for if I found love, I would not let it pass me by.'

'I cannot love her,' he said, wrestling with himself.

'You *will* not. That is a different thing. Don't let Richard's grief destroy you,' she said, stroking his cheek. 'You have been like a ghost for long enough. It is time for you to live again.'

But he only shook his head.

'If I love her, one day I will lose her. I cannot bear that pain.'

13

Helena leant back against the squabs. She felt suddenly tired, as all the excitement of the day caught up with her: waking early, finding the secret room, begging Mary for help, finding out Mary's true nature, discovering that Simon was not a monster, meeting Anna and her child, and finding her aunt.

She felt the tension that had been gripping her for the last few weeks fade away. Her muscles relaxed, and she felt at peace in a way she had not for a long time. Aunt Hester was not missing, or dead, she was safe. Helena recalled her aunt's face, cheerful and healthy, and she smiled.

The carriage left the sea behind. The cry of the gulls faded, and the tang of salt grew less marked until it disappeared altogether. The view outside the window changed from blue to green, and Helena found her thoughts moving forwards again. In a few hours she would be back at the castle, and then she would resume her masquerade as the housekeeper. She thought of revealing the truth to Mrs Beal, but it would involve divulging secrets which were not hers to tell. She would have to play her part for a little while longer.

Would Simon let her stay until her aunt returned from Italy? she wondered. Aunt Hester had seemed to think so. And yet he might ask her to leave at once. She could not bear the thought of it. He had become a part of her life, and although he had often unsettled her as well as intrigued her, she could not bear the thought of being without him.

The carriage stopped to change horses. Helena alighted, and ordered a cold collation, for she was hungry after her exertions, then she was once more on her way.

It was not long before the carriage turned off the main thoroughfare and began to cross the moors. She was nearing the castle. She looked out of the window, tracing the landmarks of her first journey: the twisted tree, the dry stone wall . . . and then the castle came in sight. It looked less threatening than it had done when she had first arrived. Then, it had been unknown. Now, it was the place where she had lived for many weeks, and although it had held terrors, it had held pleasures, too. She remembered the warm kitchen, the beauty of the ballroom, the music, waltzing with Simon in the gallery . . .

Simon! She had thought of him by his Christian name, but she had no right to call him that, not even in the privacy of her own thoughts.

Had he been in love with his sister-in-law? she wondered, or had that just been a rumour? Had he any intention of marrying Miss Fairdean, or one of the other young women at the ball? Or would he remain alone?

The carriage passed under the arch and came to a halt outside the castle. Eldridge opened the door and let down the step, and Helena climbed out. As she entered the hall, she saw signs of the ball everywhere and with a shock, she realized that it had been held only the day before. So much had happened that it seemed like a week ago. From the corridor to her left she heard the sound of tables being moved and glasses clinking. The servants were busy clearing away everything they had had to leave the night before.

Helena went to her room and removed her outdoor things, then went downstairs. She followed the sound of clinking and went into the dining-room, where a scene of chaos met her eyes. The footmen were chaffing the maids, who were making a half-hearted attempt to pile glasses on trays.

'There will be no ball this evening until the work has been finished,' she said briskly, becoming the housekeeper once again.

'Manners, take the spare chairs to the attic,' she said. 'Dawkins, take the crockery and glasses down to the kitchen, and be quick about it. All the plates and glasses have to be washed. Martha, you will have to help Effie.' Martha pulled a face. 'It is no use looking like that, this should have been done hours ago.'

'We couldn't find you . . . ' began Martha.

'That is no reason not to get on with your work. I have had other things to see to,' said Helena. 'Now, quickly. This must all be done before Lord Torkrow returns. Have any of the guests been downstairs yet?'

'No, not a one. Never get up early after a ball, that's what their servants say. Up and down they've been, with trays, though.'

'Good, it will make it easier for us to finish our work if they remain in their chambers. Once everything is finished, we can change for our ball.'

Talk of their own costume ball brightened the servants, and they became busy, clearing away the remnants of the previous night's festivities. Spare furniture was returned to the attic, the tables were cleared, cloths were removed and spirited away, the floor was swept, odd wigs, gloves and shoes were put safely aside, and the room slowly began to return to normal.

The clock struck five. The overnight guests

were now downstairs, and Helena explained to them that Lord Torkrow had been called away on urgent business, but that she had laid out a cold collation for them in the dining-room.

Some of them expressed their intention of leaving after the meal, whilst others intended to stay. They were subdued, however, and many of them were nursing sore heads and stomachs. After eating, those who did not leave the castle retired to their rooms.

Once more, the servants were free to devote their attentions to finishing clearing the ballroom, supper-room, hall and minstrels' gallery, which were littered with debris from the party, and it was seven o'clock before everything was restored to a semblance of its former state.

The remaining few guests were served supper on trays in their rooms, and then the day's work was done.

'Reckon we deserve our ball,' said Martha.

'You certainly do,' said Helena. 'A fiddler will be here in half an hour. I suggest you all go and put on your costumes, then assemble in the servants' hall.'

As the servants dispersed, Helena went upstairs to change. She did not put on her costume, having no taste for revelry, but simply changed into a clean dress. As she did so, she could not help remembering the previous night, when she had danced with Simon. As she thought of it, she remembered the feel of his fingers on hers, and the weight of his hand on her waist.

She pushed such thoughts aside and brushed her hair, then wrapped it into a neat chignon.

There was a scratching at the door, and Effie entered with a bucket of coal. She was sniffing, and when she put the bucket down, she wiped her nose with the back of her hand.

'Leave that! Go and change, or you will be late for the ball,' said Helena. 'And make sure you wash first,' she said, eyeing Effie's hands dubiously.

'Can't go. Not invited,' mumbled Effie.

'What do you mean, you're not invited? Of course you are!' said Helena. 'All the servants are invited.'

'Dawkins says it's not for scullery maids.'

'What nonsense. And besides, you are not going as a scullery maid. What costume have you chosen?'

'Haven't got one.'

'Did you not look in the chest?'

'All the lasses' costumes've gone.'

Helena felt exasperated at the girl's lack of initiative, but nevertheless she spoke kindly.

'Then we had better look in the attic. There

are chests of clothes up there. We are sure to find something to fit you. I think you should go as Cinderella. You spend your days among the cinders.'

Her humour did not make Effie smile. The girl looked more woebegone than ever.

'I couldn't, mum,' said Effie. 'Mrs Beal'd give me what for if I went through the things in the attic.'

'Not if you are with me,' said Helena.

Then, taking Effie firmly by the hand — the one the girl had not used for wiping her nose — she led her up to the attic and together they looked through an old trunk.

'Now, what do you think of this?' she asked, as she held out a panniered gown.

'I couldn't wear nothing like that. That's for a lady,' said Effie.

'Tonight, you are a lady,' said Helena. She picked up the dress, and led the girl downstairs again. 'Now, you just have a wash.'

Effie needed a great deal of encouragement, but in the end she stripped down to her chemise. Helena breathed a sigh of relief when she saw it was clean. Mrs Beal evidently took a motherly interest in the girl. Then Effie washed at Helena's washstand, before putting on the gown. Helena helped her to fasten it, before turning Effie round so that she could see herself in the cheval glass.

'You look beautiful,' said Helena.

Effie looked at herself in amazement.

'Like a real lady,' she said, plucking at the dress in wonder.

'Here,' said Helena, handing her a wig. 'You will be Lady . . . ' she trailed away, then asked, 'What is your favourite name?'

'Charlotte,' said Effie promptly.

'Then tonight you will be Lady Charlotte. If anyone asks, you must give that as your name.'

Effie scratched her head, knocking her wig and giving it a lopsided appearance. Helena straightened it again and said, 'No scratching.'

'No, mum.'

'Now, go downstairs, Lady Charlotte, and enjoy yourself.'

Effie walked out of the chamber, picking up the bucket of coal as she passed.

'Not tonight, Effie. I will see to the fires,' said Helena.

She took the bucket of coal and put it back on the hearth.

She waited for Effie to reach the end of the corridor, and then followed her, to make sure the other servants did not tease her, but she need not have worried. There was already a mood of jollity in the servants' hall, and Effie was swept into a dance by a young man dressed as a pirate. Who he was, Helena did not know. One of the footmen, probably. There seemed to be an awful lot of them, and she guessed that some of the visiting servants and possibly some of the villagers had sneaked into the ball under cover of a costume. A few extra tankards of ale would be drunk, and a few extra sandwiches eaten, but no harm would be done. In fact, some good might come out of it, because the villagers might lose some of their superstitious fear of Simon and the castle.

The fiddler was scraping his bow across his fiddle, and stamping his foot to provide a drum. Helena found herself caught round the waist, and was soon whirling round with the other dancers, not stopping until her partner released her to get a tankard of ale.

'Well, this is fun and no mistake,' said Mrs Beal, joining her at the side of the room. Mrs Beal was dressed, in rather unlikely fashion, as a nymph. 'This dress is very tight,' she complained, 'but it was the only costume left.' She surveyed the dancers. 'Who's the young girl in the panniered gown?'

'That's Effie,' said Helena.

'Why, bless my soul, the girl's light on her feet. I never would have thought it. Just look at her!'

Effie was lifted from the floor by her partner, then dropped carefully back to the ground, where she twirled lightly around before swapping partners.

'There'll be some surprised faces when she takes her mask off,' said Mrs Beal. 'Is everyone here?'

'Eldridge is not coming.'

'That doesn't surprise me. He's never been one for fun and games.' She looked round again, then said, 'I'd best encourage everyone to eat something. There's a deal of ale being drunk. We don't want sore heads in the morning.'

Helena left the noise of the dance, and went upstairs. She looked into the main rooms and made sure the fires were ablaze, for Lord Torkrow would be cold when he returned home.

The long-case clock in the library struck ten o'clock.

He could be here soon, she thought. The ship sailed at seven o'clock.

She hoped that all had gone well, and that Anna and George had set sail, escaping England and Morton for ever.

She went over to the window and pulled back the curtains. The moon was high, and cast a silvery glow into the world below. The stars were out, and it was a magical scene.

The moors, which had once seemed threatening, now seemed serene.

The room overlooked the front of the castle, and she strained her eyes, hoping to see a speck in the distance, something moving, which could be a carriage, but she could see nothing. She sat on the window seat, with her knees pulled up in front of her and her arms wrapped round them. She was at last rewarded. In the distance, she caught sight of movement. Simon was coming!

He must not find her in his library. She had no right to wait for him. She must return to the ball.

She left the window seat and pulled the curtains, then went out into the hall. She was halfway across when one of the footmen, dressed as a cavalier emerged from the direction of the kitchen. His costume gave him a swagger, and it was not surprising, thought Helena. His bucket boots, with their deep turned-over tops, were made for swaggering, and so was the extravagant costume, with its doublet and breeches in bright blue satin, and its falling collar of white lace. He wore a short cloak, which he had thrown back over one of his shoulders in a careless attitude. Over his face he wore a black silk mask, and on his head was a wide-brimmed hat with an extravagant plume.

'Are you taking the air?' she asked him.

He raised his hand, and she saw that he was holding a pistol.

'You have picked the wrong person to rob,' she said, entering into the spirit of the masquerade. 'I have no money.'

He said nothing, and something about his stance made her falter. The hairs on the back of her neck rose, and she had the unsettling thought that the pistol could be loaded.

'You thought you were very clever,' he said.

She felt a chill as she heard his voice. She had heard it before, in Mary's cottage. The man before her was Morton. But what was he doing here? How did he get in?

She had no time to wonder. He was walking towards her.

She began to back away from him. There was a bell on the wall behind her. In the confusion of the evening its summons might be ignored, but it might be answered, if only she could reach it.

'What do you want? How did you get here?' she asked, hoping to distract him so that he would not see what she was doing.

'You know what I want. I want my wife and son.'

'Your wife and son are dead, killed by you and your cruelty. You can see their gravestone

286

in Hull. They died shortly after they arrived there.'

'I've already seen the gravestone. I've dug up the ground beneath it, too, and seen there was nothing there.'

'What?' gasped Helena, horrified that he would do such a thing.

'There were no bodies. My wife and son are not dead. He's hidden them somewhere, and you are going to tell me where.'

'I don't know,' said Helena.

'You were in Hull today.'

'I was abandoned before I got there,' she said. 'Your sister — or should I say, mistress — left me at the inn.'

'But you found your way there with Simon. Don't bother to deny it. I saw his carriage leaving Hull with you inside. At the time I was more interested in finding my wife and child. But after following the false scent laid by my dear brother-in-law, then returning to the Vances to punish them for telling me lies, only to find they had fled in the meantime, I decided to visit the castle and find out what I want to know.'

'How did you get in?'

'Simon hasn't changed his habits. The kitchen door was unlocked, and the servants' costume ball was about to begin. A mask, a wig, and a cavalier's clothes let me pass unnoticed. You've been elusive. I thought I would find you downstairs. But it seems you have lost your taste for dancing. You are waiting for Simon, I suppose. And I — I am waiting for an answer to my question. Where are my wife and child?'

'You will never find them,' she said.

He took off his mask and his face was hard.

'Believe me, I will.' He levelled his pistol. 'Now where are they?'

'You would do better to leave them alone. They do not want you,' she returned.

'They do not have a choice in the matter. They are my property. They belong to me.'

To her surprise, she heard Simon's voice cut through the air, and she felt a wave of relief as she realized that he had arrived.

'My housekeeper does not know where they are. I sent her home so that she would not be involved. I have put Anna and the boy beyond your reach, somewhere you will never find them. Now drop the pistol.'

Morton turned and levelled the pistol at Simon instead.

'Not until you tell me where they are.'

'That I will never do,' said Simon, walking forward.

Morton cocked the pistol.

'What good will it do to shoot me?' asked Simon. 'If you kill me, you will never find out what you want to know.'

'I will never find out if you live. I know you, Simon. You'd rather die than see your precious sister resume her duties as my wife, so I might as well kill you,' said Morton.

'Then do it,' said Simon.

'No!' cried Helena.

Morton turned the pistol back to her, but he spoke to Simon.

'You might play with your life, but I'll wager you won't play with anyone else's.'

'You're bluffing,' said Simon. 'You have only one shot in that pistol. If you shoot her, I will be on you, and I will make sure you pay for your crime.'

'You've gambled with me often enough to know that I don't bluff,' said Morton. 'Besides' — he pulled a second pistol from his cloak — 'I have two pistols. One for her, and one for you. So tell me, Simon, are you willing to let her die? If you are, say nothing. If not, then tell me where Anna is. I'll let her go, and you will have saved your housekeeper's life. You might save Anna's life as well, if you can reach her before me. No one has to die here tonight.'

'Don't listen to him,' said Helena.

Simon's eyes turned to her, and she saw something in them she had not expected: she saw fear.

'I cannot let him kill you,' he said.

And then there came the sound of another pistol cocking behind her, and all three of them stopped in surprise. Helena caught sight of the mirror on the wall. She was standing in the centre of the hall. Morton was levelling a pistol at her. Between them and the front door was Simon. But standing behind Morton, almost invisible in the shadows, was Miss Parkins, and she was holding a pistol to his head. 'You will never have my lady's child,' she said, and her voice was as dead as a sepulchre.

Morton recovered his composure.

'If you pull the trigger, you will kill me, but not before I kill her,' he said.

'Do you think I care about her? A servant?' said Miss Parkins. 'I care about one thing, and one thing alone: the oath I swore to my lady. I promised her I would care for her children. It was I who nursed Miss Anna as she lay feverishly in the castle, brought low by your whippings, and when I saw what you had done to her, I swore that one day I would have the whipping of you.'

She stood there like an avenging demon, and Morton faltered. Helena saw it, and without thinking she knocked the pistol out of his raised hand. He lifted his other hand, but Simon was upon him and wresting the second pistol from him, sending it hurtling to the floor.

'Damn you!' said Morton, as Simon held him fast.

'There will be no bloodshed here,' said Simon to Miss Parkins. 'Give me your weapon.'

She did not respond.

'Anna is safe. Now give me the pistol.'

Slowly Miss Parkins handed it to him, and he put it in his pocket.

Helena breathed again. She was about to pick up the two dropped pistols when a voice came from the shadows.

'Let him go.'

Morton looked round and saw Maria standing there. He wrenched himself free of Simon and ran over to her. He was about to take the pistol she was holding out to him when there was a loud crack! and Helena turned in astonishment to see that Miss Parkins was wielding a whip. It flicked around Maria's wrist . . . Maria, shocked, jerked her hand in an attempt to get it free . . . the pistol went off . . . everyone froze with shock . . . and then Morton's hands rose to his chest as a look of surprise spread across his face.

When he removed his hands, they were covered in blood.

'No!' cried Maria, as he began to fall.

She caught him, and his weight dragged her to her knees.

Helena looked on in horror as Morton's blood seeped across the flagstones.

'Don't leave me!' said Maria.

'Never thought . . . you . . . would be the one to kill me,' he said to her in surprise.

Then his eyes closed, and Maria began to cry.

Helena stood rooted to the spot. It had all happened so quickly that she was still having difficulty in taking it in. It was only a few minutes since she had been sitting in the library, looking forward to Simon's return, and now here she was in the hall, with Morton dead at her feet. Simon was rooted, too. But Miss Parkins was fully in command of herself.

She had the whip all ready, thought Helena, recalling Miss Parkins's words: 'When I saw what you had done to her, I swore that one day I would have the whipping of you.' *She must have seen Morton arrive, and come to the hall prepared to carry out her threat.*

'Something must be done,' said Miss Parkins.

Simon shook himself, as though clearing his head.

'She must be charged with murder,' said Miss Parkins, looking balefully at Maria.

Maria did not even look up, but went on weeping.

'No,' said Simon, taking the whip from Miss Parkins and coiling it round his hand. 'I will not have Anna's name tainted with scandal, and so the true circumstances of the evening must never come out. Anna has a chance now to come home and to live in England, where she can raise George in peace and safety, and where, when he is older, he can claim his inheritance. I will not have his future ruined by this night's work.'

'What do you mean to do?' asked Helena, looking at him.

'I don't know. I have not decided yet. Say that Morton's death was an accident, perhaps.'

'She will never let your sister live in peace,' said Miss Parkins, her eyes still on Maria.

Helena looked at Maria and saw that she had become quieter. Her sobbing had all but ceased, and now she sat quietly on the floor, looking at the man in her arms.

'I think she will,' said Helena. 'She has too much to lose if she tells the truth.'

Simon nodded.

'Maria,' he said.

Maria turned red-rimmed eyes on him.

'If you give me your word you will never return to Stormcrow Castle and that you will never harm any member of my family, then I will see to it that you go free.'

She nodded dully.

'You give me your word?'

'Yes,' she said.

'Very well,' said Simon. He thought. 'Then we will say this: that you were my house guest; that you expressed an interest in learning to shoot; that Morton said he would teach you; that your aim went wide, and that you shot him by mistake. Do you understand?'

'I do.'

'Good. Then I will send Eldridge for the undertaker. I will send for Sir Hugh Greer, too. I do not want anyone to suspect that anything is amiss.' He turned to Miss Parkins. 'I need you to get Maria out of the hall — '

'You can put her in the housekeeper's room,' said Helena.

Simon agreed. 'And Morton's body, too. We don't want any of the servants coming upstairs and stumbling across it.'

Miss Parkins inclined her head.

He turned to Helena, and saying, 'Wait for me in the library. I would like to speak to you when I return,' he set off for the stables.

Helena walked across the hall, her body

feeling heavy. A reaction was starting to set in, and she felt cold. She went into the library, where the fire cast a mellow glow over the furniture and the clock ticked contentedly on the mantelpiece. To her surprise, she saw that only a quarter of an hour had passed since she had been sitting there last, waiting for Simon's return.

She went over to the fire and knelt down in front of it, feeling glad of its warmth. She thought over everything that had happened, until the jumble of images at last began to resolve themselves into an orderly pattern, and she felt her lethargy leave her.

It was some time before Simon joined her. As he entered the library she could see there were lines of strain on his face. She stood up, lifting her hand to soothe them away, but then dropped it again, for she knew she must not touch him.

'I have sent for Sir Hugh,' he said.

'How is Maria?' she asked.

'Still quiet.'

'Do you trust her?' asked Helena.

'No. I think it possible that, once she recovers from Morton's death, she will want revenge, so I propose to have her watched, to make sure she can do no more harm.'

'What will happen now?' asked Helena.

'We will hold the funeral as soon as

possible. Morton has no family, so I propose to bury him here. He is my brother-in-law, and it will not seem too strange that I should do so. The funeral will be a quiet affair. I doubt if many people will come, for my neighbours did not know him, and I do not intend to noise it abroad: the sooner it is dealt with, the better.'

'I understand.'

There came the sound of voices from the hall, and the sound of footsteps: Sir Hugh Greer had arrived.

'I must leave you,' said Simon, stepping back.

The door was thrown open and Sir Hugh strode into the room, blowing into his hands.

'Now then, Pargeter, what's all this? There's been an accident, I understand.'

'Yes.'

'It's a good thing your man found me on the road or he wouldn't have got hold of me until tomorrow. I'm due at the Bancrofts' in an hour, so you'll have to be quick. What's happened?'

'Unfortunately, my brother-in-law has been shot. He was showing one of my guests, a lady, how to fire a pistol. She had never held one before, and although she did her best to follow his instructions, her aim went wide.'

'Dead?' asked Sir Hugh succinctly.

'Dead.'

'Never put a gun into the hands of a woman,' said Sir Hugh, shaking his head. 'They mean well, bless 'em, but it's asking for trouble.'

As the two men talked, Helena resumed her role as the housekeeper and quietly withdrew.

14

It was a cold, dreary day when Morton was buried. As Simon had foreseen, few people attended the funeral, and none of them accompanied him back to the castle afterwards, although he had been scrupulous about asking them. There had been a little gossip, but it had soon been overtaken as a subject of interest by news of Mrs Willis's expectation of a happy event.

'We all thought her husband was too old,' said Mrs Beal to Helena at breakfast a few days later, 'but there, she'll be delighted, poor thing. Always wanted children, she did. 'It must be awful to be alone in the world,' she said to me once. She was thinking of it even then. Two years married and not a sign of a child. But now ... yes, it's a happy event.'

Helena thought of Mrs Willis and the young man at the ball, and then she thought of Mrs Willis's strange words when they had taken tea together — *It was a pity she was all alone in the world, with no one to miss her when she was gone* — and knew now that Mrs Willis had not been thinking her aunt was an easy target for wrongdoing, as she had suspected at the time, but had simply been thinking of her own situation.

Helena finished her breakfast and then went to the housekeeper's room to start on the day's work. As she went in, she saw *Le Morte D'Arthur* sitting on her desk, and she picked it up, meaning to return it to the library, for she had finished it. As she did so, she thought about the many forms love could take: the courtly love of her book, Maria's love for Morton, Simon's love for Anna, Anna's love for her son.

And then she thought about her own love: her love for her parents, her love for Caroline, her love for aunt . . . and her love for Simon. She could no longer hide it from herself; she was in love with him.

She was crossing the hall when she saw Miss Parkins coming down the stairs. Miss Parkins was dressed in her outdoor clothes, with a long grey cloak covering her bony body, and in her hand was a valise.

'Are you going out?' asked Helena in surprise.

Miss Parkins turned calm eyes on her, and Helena was surprised at the change in them. They looked human at last. Her face had smoothed, as though she had been holding herself rigid for a long time and had finally allowed herself to relax.

'My time here is done,' she said.

'You don't mean you're leaving?' asked Helena in surprise.

'I have done what I promised. I have looked after my lady's children. Her oldest son I could not save; he was dead before I made my vow. But her remaining children will now be happy. Her daughter is rid of a monstrous brute, and her younger son . . . I blamed him for a time, but now all is forgiven. I have forgiven him, and he has forgiven himself.' Miss Parkins walked towards the door, then turned and said, 'I wish you well.'

There was a flicker of a smile in her eyes and Helena saw in her a completely different person; not a terrifying, unnatural mannequin, but a devoted woman who had loved her mistress and who had loved her mistress's children.

It seemed strange to think she had been so frightened of Miss Parkins when she had arrived at the castle, for now she knew that, although Miss Parkins had been alarming, she had been dangerous only to those who had threatened the Pargeters, and had been dangerous to Helena only whilst she had thought that Helena was a threat.

'And I you,' said Helena. 'Where will you go?'

'To my sister. She lives in Dorset. It is where we grew up. I am looking forward to going home.'

★   ★   ★

Simon stood on the landing, watching Miss Parkins through the window as she climbed into the carriage and set out on her journey. She had been a part of his life ever since he could remember. She had given him a sense of security in his childhood, for she had always been there, always the same . . . until the day his sister-in-law had died.

He remembered how Miss Parkins had blamed him; not for the death of his sister-in-law, nor even the death of his brother, but for the way Richard's death had killed his mother.

But now Miss Parkins had forgiven him. And she was right, he thought, as he remembered the words he had overheard, he had forgiven himself. It was as though a great burden had been lifted from him, and now that it was gone, he could look to the future again. A future with Helena.

He began to walk downstairs. He had been determined never to fall in love, because love led to loss, and loss led to pain. But something had happened to him when Morton had turned the pistol on Helena. He had known in that moment that it was impossible to avoid love, because love had found him anyway. But he had known something else, too: that, terrible though it would be to lose Helena, it would be better than never having loved her, because the joy and the pleasure of loving her had been worth any pain.

And now he wanted to tell her so.

*   *   *

Helena returned *Le Morte D'Arthur* to its place on the bookshelves and was about to leave the library when Simon walked in. He stopped and looked at her with such intensity that her hands clenched and unclenched themselves. He seemed about to speak, but then he closed his mouth and walked over to her until he was standing in front of her, so close that the front of his coat was touching the front of her dress. She could feel the warmth of his breath on her cheeks and she felt as though something momentous was about to happen.

'Helena . . . there is so much I want to say to you . . . ' he began.

She turned up her face to his expectantly

and saw the words die on his lips. His head came closer and her own tilted in response. And then he kissed her.

And her heart quaked.

★   ★   ★

'I suppose it is too much to hope that the villagers will stop calling you Stormcrow,' she said, as they walked outside in the garden some hours later. Though the day was dull, it was fine, and it felt good to be out of doors.

'It is. But it is not a bad name, and when our children are old enough, I will tell them so.'

She looked at him and he took her hands in his.

'Helena, I'm in love with you. Will you marry me?' he said.

'Yes, Simon, I will.'

He smiled, a natural smile, with no shadows in it, then he put his arm around her and they walked on.

'A stormcrow brings warning of a storm, it is true, but it also flies before the storm and, in the end, outraces it,' he said. 'We are all stormcrows, each one of us, for we all, at some time, bring bad news. But whilst I had to tell my brother that his wife was dead, and my mother that her son had died, I was also

303

the bearer of good news, for I told my sister she was free. Our children will have their own storms and their own sanctuaries in the course of their lives, their own good news and bad.'

'And, if they are lucky, they will find their own loves, as we have,' said Helena.

She thought of the first time she had seen Simon. She had had no idea, when he had taken her up in his carriage, that she would fall in love with him. It had come upon her so slowly that she could not pinpoint the day or the time when it had happened, but it was now so much a part of her existence that she could no longer conceive of life without him.

> *'A long, long kiss, a kiss of youth, and love,*
> *And beauty, all concentrating like rays*
> *Into one focus, kindled from above . . .*
> *Each kiss a heart quake . . .*

'I never thought I would find it, that kind of love, nor my place in the world,' she said, 'but here it is, at Stormcrow Castle, with you.'

We do hope that you have enjoyed reading this large print book.

Did you know that all of our titles are available for purchase?

We publish a wide range of high quality large print books including:
Romances, Mysteries, Classics
General Fiction
Non Fiction and Westerns

Special interest titles available in large print are:
The Little Oxford Dictionary
Music Book
Song Book
Hymn Book
Service Book

Also available from us courtesy of Oxford University Press:
Young Readers' Dictionary
(large print edition)
Young Readers' Thesaurus
(large print edition)

For further information or a free brochure, please contact us at:
Ulverscroft Large Print Books Ltd.,
The Green, Bradgate Road, Anstey,
Leicester, LE7 7FU, England.
Tel: (00 44) 0116 236 4325
Fax: (00 44) 0116 234 0205

HARSTAIRS HOUSE

Amanda Grange

When Susannah Thorpe inherits Harstairs House, she finds more than she bargains for, as the house has a tenant in the broodingly handsome shape of Oliver Bristow. With only a month left on his lease, Susannah allows him to remain, but a series of unexplained incidents causes her to question Oliver's motives for staying. Susannah's search to discover the answer to this mystery results in her being swept into an adventure that changes her life. Ultimately, one burning question still remains — now that his tenancy is over, will Oliver stay?

TR
LR

1	31	61	91	121	151	181	211	241	271	301	331
2	32	62	92	122	152	182	212	242	272	302	332
3	33	63	93	123	153	183	213	243	273	303	333
4	34	64	94	124	154	184	214	244	274	304	334
5	35	65	95	125	155	185	215	245	275	305	335
6	36	66	96	126	156	186	216	246	276	306	336
7	37	67	97	127	157	187	217	247	277	307	337
8	38	68	98	128	158	188	218	248	278	308	338
9	39	69	99	129	159	189	219	249	279	309	339
10	40	70	100	130	160	190	220	250	280	310	340
11	41	71	101	131	161	191	221	251	281	311	341
12	42	72	102	132	162	192	222	252	282	312	342
13	43	73	103	133	163	193	223	253	283	313	343
14	44	74	104	134	164	194	224	254	284	314	344
15	45	75	105	135	165	195	225	255	285	315	345
16	46	76	106	136	166	196	226	256	286	316	346
17	47	77	107	137	167	197	227	257	287	317	347
18	48	78	108	138	168	198	228	258	288	318	348
19	49	79	109	139	169	199	229	259	289	319	349
20	50	80	110	140	170	200	230	260	290	320	350
21	51	81	111	141	171	201	231	261	291	321	351
22	52	82	112	142	172	202	232	262	292	322	352
23	53	83	113	143	173	203	233	263	293	323	353
24	54	84	114	144	174	204	234	264	294	324	354
25	55	85	115	145	175	205	235	265	295	325	355
26	56	86	116	146	176	206	236	266	296	326	356
27	57	87	117	147	177	207	237	267	297	327	357
28	58	88	118	148	178	208	238	268	298	328	358
29	59	89	119	149	179	209	239	269	299	329	359
30	60	90	120	150	180	210	240	270	300	330	360